From the forgotten queens of sci-fi and horror pulps, to vignettes of Black life in Chicago in the late 1950s, to time-traveling and galaxy-hopping puns, our Beyond Pulp Reprints series brings neglected works back into print in editions that are both attractive and affordable.

STRANGE AWAKENING

A NOVEL BY DOROTHY QUICK

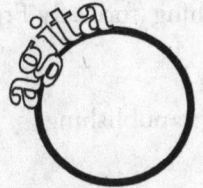

Book design and layout by Michael W. Phillips Jr.

Published by Agita Publishing (formerly From Beyond Press)
agitapublishing.com
mike@agitapublishing.com
Instagram & Bluesky: @agitapublishing

ISBN: 979-8-9925941-1-9
Library of Congress Control Number: 2026930003
Agita edition, June 2026

To Mother

If I could take the roses of a June
Distill their fragrance into magic words
Containing the bright glory of high noon
And the lush notes of all the singing birds,
Then capture gleaming star dust from the skies
To weave in sentences pristinely new—
With words like these and time to make me wise
I could write something worthier of you.

— Dorothy Quick

Contents

By Some Strange Agency:
Dorothy Quick and *Strange Awakening*

Dorothy Quick was one of the most prolific and talented women writers of weird fiction in the heyday of the pulps in the first half of the twentieth century. But she's remembered today, if at all, for her childhood friendship with Mark Twain. My hope is that the re-publication of this, her only science fiction novel, will help restore her reputation as one of the early masters of speculative fiction.

She was born Dorothy Gertrude Quick on September 1, 1896, the daughter of Gertrude and Henry Stanhope Quick Jr., who worked in the shipping industry. The family lived either in New Jersey or at 300 Park Avenue in Manhattan, depending on the source you consult.

Quick met Mark Twain on a steamship in 1907, when she was eleven and he was seventy-two. She became one of his "angelfish": young children—mostly girls—whom he befriended and mentored, perhaps because he had no grandchildren of his own. Their close friendship lasted until his death in 1910. Toward the end of her life, Dorothy published a memoir of her time with Twain. Originally called *Enchantment: A Little Girl's Friendship with Mark Twain*, the memoir was adapted into the 1991 movie *Mark Twain and Me*.

Viewed through the lens of today, Twain's friendship with Quick and the other angelfish was a tad inappropriate. They would stay with him, unchaperoned except for his household servants, for days at a time. His letters border on the obsessive: "I went to bed as soon as you departed, there being nothing to live for after that, and the sunshine all gone. How do you suppose I am going to get along without you?" A review of Ron Chernow's biography of Twain in

The Nation said, "It was all very chaste, but his was an obsession with creatures of imagined innocence, before they grew to the age of the complex, troubled adult women in his household."[1]

The two formed an "author's league," and Twain gave Quick invaluable advice that she credited for turning her into a successful writer. "If you ever take to verse making," he wrote, "be sure your poems are short and have something in them that will make people take notice. That will keep them awake, and then they'll be sure to remember you, dear."[2]

However, his advice was sometimes domineering. Quick sent a story to a contest sponsored by *St. Nicholas*—a magazine that had published the childhood writings of Edna St. Vincent Millay, F. Scott Fitzgerald, and E.B. White—and received an honorable mention. Instead of praising her achievement, Twain disapproved: "Dear heart, you mustn't send stories to *St. Nicholas* yet. It is too soon. You must learn the trade first and nobody can do that without a long and diligent apprenticeship—not anything short of ten years. Write the stories, write lots and lots of them for practice." She followed his advice. "I waited much more than the prescribed ten years before I sent out a story again!"[3]

Quick was a talented singer, and she was inspired by Twain's daughter Clara, whose musical aspirations were belittled by her famous father. When Quick told her mentor that she wanted to study music, he opposed the plan vehemently: "You little rascal! I won't accept your resignation from the Authors' League at this point... You can't change a career as easily as you change your mind, even if you are feminine!" And he struck the bannister to emphasize his disapproval. "To do one thing well will take all your time. You must have a goal to make and follow the path directly to it. You can do lots of things to help you towards it, but you can't have two goals. You can't be a writer and a singer." Tellingly, he finished with, "Besides, I can't teach you singing."

1. Quick, *Mark Twain & Me* (University of Oklahoma Press, 1961), p. 79; Adam Horchschild, "The Adventures of Samuel Clemens," *The Nation*, August 11, 2025. https://www.thenation.com/article/culture/mark-twain-ron-chernow

2. *Mark Twain & Me*, p. 91.

3. *Mark Twain & Me*, p. 105.

She set aside her dream, at least temporarily.[4]

Quick was devastated after Twain's death in April 1910, and she gave up writing:

> For many years I refused to let the idea of writing come back into my thoughts. I studied singing after I graduated from school with the idea of an operatic career, for there was an urge in me that demanded some medium of expression. But all the time there was a murmur in the back of my mind, a whispering that would not be silent, for the memory of what Mark Twain had said kept drawing me back to the thing he had wanted me to do. Like the recurrent pull of the undertow, it was ever present in the depths of my being, and I could not shut it away.[5]

At some point between 1910 and 1919, Quick's parents divorced, and her mother married seventy-six-year-old financier Thomas Jefferson Mumford. Before he died in 1924, Mumford willed $3 million in stocks to his wife and stepdaughter. In 1927, trustees of his estate sued Dorothy and her mother, alleging that Gertrude had taken advantage of her husband's failing health and convinced him to modify his will. I can find no record of how the suit played out, but given Mrs. Mumford's continued existence in the society pages and on the donor lists of charitable institutions, I think it's safe to say that she won.[6]

After the divorce, Quick's father lived with his unmarried sister Amelia in Brooklyn. On May 12, 1935, Amelia died of a heart attack; when Henry was informed of her death, he also died of a heart attack.

In 1925, Quick married John Adams Mayer. A composer and insurance agent, he had graduated from the U.S. Naval Academy and served in the U.S. Navy during World War I, where his service was recognized by the Romanian government. *Time Magazine* ran an item announcing the engagement, and the *New*

4. *Mark Twain & Me*, p. 126
5. *Mark Twain & Me*, p. 218.
6. *New York Times*, October 12, 1927.

York Herald-Tribune ran a story about their wedding, which was held at Quick's mother's home. A Romanian prince and a British baron attended.[7]

Quick was in poor health throughout her life. Her memoir of Twain is littered with lengthy bouts of bronchitis, which left her convalescing in bed for weeks at a time. "You are a frail little creature," Twain wrote her, "and you need to get away from doctors and let generous and wise nature build you up and make you strong." A 1938 *New York Post* article reported that "for the past year she has been confined to her home for quite extended periods," possibly recuperating from appendicitis. She said elsewhere that she started writing stories to deal with the boredom of her extended illnesses.[8]

Quick returned to writing in the 1920s. In 1925, Broadway impresario John Cort staged her play *The Pool*, and 1927 saw the publication of *Threads*, the first of her eight poetry collections. And, most importantly for our purposes, in 1932 she sold a story to *Oriental Stories*, editor Farnsworth Wright's sister publication to *Weird Tales*. This launched her career as a prolific writer of weird fiction. Over the next twenty years, she would publish twenty-three stories and twenty-five poems in pulp horror and sci-fi magazines. And in 1938, she published her only science fiction novel, *Strange Awakening*. More on that later.

In the late 1940s, Quick branched out into cozy mysteries, and she was good at it. *The Fifth Dagger* (1947) is a fun locked-room murder mystery in which a plucky young bride, Diana Blakeley, helps solve a string of murders in posh Boston society. The plot is a howler, but in a fun way: Honora Davenport, a gorgeous and mentally unbalanced young woman, is obsessed with Diana's husband Alan, Honora's former psychiatrist. When Honora is murdered at a soirée (with the first of the five daggers), suspicion falls on the good doctor. As the bodies pile up and the police close in on Dr. Blakeley, Diana must crack the case before all five daggers find their homes in people's vital organs. It's a solid proto-feminist mystery, well told, with sufficient twists and turns that I was unable to figure out the solution before Quick revealed it. (Of course, I never

---

7. *East Hampton Star*, March 21, 1940
8. *Mark Twain & Me*, p. 163; *New York Post*, January 24, 1938.

figure out mysteries early—I love being baffled by a good puzzle.) Quick wrote several more mysteries, some featuring Diana Blakeley, and I think they're worth a look.

She also wrote several plays, but I could track down only one. *One Night in Holyrood* (1949) is a one-act historical drama about Mary, Queen of Scots. It takes place on the night after her second husband, Lord Darnley, had her close friend, secretary, and possible lover David Rizzio murdered. The play is in artless iambic pentameter, and I could definitely see parallels between the verse in the play and Quick's poetry.

Throughout her life, Quick was a respected writer. Most of her poetry collections and mysteries were reviewed in major newspapers. In 1958, she was part of a panel discussion, "The Nature of Writing and Publishing a Book," with John Steinbeck, John O'Hara, and P.G. Wodehouse. Until the end of her life, Quick continued publishing novels and poetry books and writing plays and songs, many of which were performed by luminaries of the New York theater and music scenes.[9]

For nearly forty years, Quick spent her summers in the Hamptons on Long Island. A local newspaper profile of her informs us that she "starts work at 9am daily, typing her stories in her room surrounded by cages of pet canary birds, interrupted at intervals by her fox terrier, Musty, and her bashful Skye terrier, Suzy."[10] From 1940 until her death, she wrote a weekly column for the *East Hampton Star* called "What's New in New York" about life in the big city. Topics included reviews of plays and movies she'd seen, biographies of local poets, her view that dogs are better than cats (editor's note: she's wrong), whether you should help a baby bird that's fallen out of its nest (with input from the director of the New York Zoological Society), and air raid preparations during World War II.

What struck me when reading a sampling of the columns, and indeed throughout my research on her, is that she was a very private person despite appearing in the society gossip pages whenever she attended the opera or dined at a fancy restaurant. While I didn't read every column, I failed to find much about her as a person. She

---

9. *New York Times*, May 18, 1958.
10. *East Hampton Star*, November 14, 1940.

didn't miss a week when her husband died suddenly at the age of forty-eight in 1940, nor did she mention his death in her column. The same thing happened when her mother died in 1942. Both are surprising, but the latter is especially so: Her mother appears to have been both parent and best friend, and each of Quick's books is dedicated "To Mother."

Quick continued suffering from poor health, and after 1959, she could no longer make her annual trip to the Hamptons. Her last column in the *East Hampton Star* appeared in early March 1962; in it, she talked about her excitement about astronaut John Glenn's orbit of the Earth the month before:

> What a world we live in, and how grateful we should be that science has achieved such marvels, and how we should put forth all our efforts to prevent the destruction of our wonderful world…after this, anything I can write will be an anti-climax, but "the show must go on," so here I go.[11]

Then she wrote about pangolins at the Bronx Zoo.

Dorothy Gertrude Quick Mayer died at her Manhattan home, which overlooked Central Park, on March 15, 1962. She's buried alongside her mother in her stepfather's tomb in New Jersey.

Strange Awakening

Strange Awakening was published in 1938 by House of Field, which appeared to specialize in biographies and autobiographies, including works by patent attorney Louis Chayka, financier Lyman Gage, and Rita Olcott, the widow of actor Chauncey Olcott.

Those names are likely unfamiliar now, and may have been even in the 1930s and 1940s. It seems that House of Field was a hybrid publisher, where authors subsidize the publication of their books. An exposé of proprietor Rudolph Field's lurid divorce described his business model as "putting out books for amateurs so anxious to see their work and names in print that they are willing to finance it."[12]

---

11. *East Hampton Star*, March 8, 1962.

12. *St. Louis Post-Dispatch*, March 12, 1944.

That may explain how chintzy the first and only edition of *Strange Awakening* is. Although most hardcovers of the day had pictorial dust jackets, Quick's book was plain, bearing only the title and her name—misspelled as "Dorthy Quick." It's unclear how many House of Field authors paid Field to publish their books, and it's possible that Quick, the stepdaughter of a wealthy financier, was one of them.

Unlike Quick's mysteries, which were reviewed in prominent newspapers, *Strange Awakening* attracted little attention. The only contemporary review I found was from the *Prairie Schooner*, where reviewer Mary Maddock said:

> If you like to get away from a dull life, if you want to live excitingly in another world when you read fiction, then *Strange Awakening* is your book! One hesitates to call it a fantasy, because the characters who people *Strange Awakening* are just as real as the people next door—more real because in the end you know and like them a whole lot better.[13]

The book is about Iva, a girl from Long Island who is magically transported to Venus by its despotic ruler, the Great Mind, who wants to violate her chastity because he's bored with Venusian women. But one of his lieutenants, Ota of the Blue People, finds her first and falls in love with her. He decides to rebel against the Great Mind so he can marry Iva.

It's an example of a sub-genre of science fiction called "planetary romance," a cousin of space opera. And the emphasis here is on romance: I've been pitching the novel as John Carter of Mars meets *Alices's Adventures in Wonderland*, but with more kissing, and I stand by that. It harks back to an earlier, more innocent phase in science fiction, where it doesn't matter how Iva came to Venus, how the various bits of Venusian technology function, or how, exactly, Iva and Ota could be physically compatible. Instead, the emphasis is on vivid description, adventure, and a sense of wonder.

---

13. *Prairie Schooner*, Summer 1938.

Acknowledgements

Thanks, as always, to Eric Williams, editor of *Night Fears: Weird Tales in Translation*, and Bobby Derie of Deep Cuts in a Lovecraftian Vein for answering my questions, pointing me in the direction of sources, and talking through my reprint projects. Thanks to Jaclyn Youhana Garver, my co-editor on *Requiem for a Siren: Women Poets of the Pulps*, for editing this introduction and listening to me geek out over Dorothy Quick. And thanks, as always, to Interlibrary Loan.

—*Michael W. Phillips Jr.*

Chapter I
A Restless Night

For some strange reason Iva couldn't sleep. In all of the nineteen years of her life she had never been troubled by sleeplessness before. But tonight she tossed and turned on her crepe de chine sheets in a vain effort to woo Morpheus.

The Long Island village had long since settled into slumber and as it was the middle of the week, there were no late revellers returning to their homes to break the stillness. A great mantle of silence had descended over everything, only broken by the soft lapping of the Ocean as it came gently up upon the beach.

Iva raised herself on one elbow and looked out at the sea from the casement windows that ran alongside her bed. It was a beautiful night with a full moon. The moonlight flooded the water and streamed in Iva's windows. The stars seemed to have a peculiar radiance of their own—one in particular was very bright.

Iva played with the idea of drawing the curtains but then dismissed the thought. "It's too beautiful to shut out," she said half aloud; "Besides, I'd know it was there." She relaxed back on to the pillows and lying flat on her back found she could still see the star that she had noticed before. It appeared to her unnaturally large, but then she knew nothing of Astronomy.

The soft summer breeze blew her golden curls about her forehead, but it did not lull her to sleep. The big blue eyes with their heavy black lashes remained open, fixed upon the shining radiance of the gleaming star.

The crepe de chine sheet outlined the slender figure and the moonlight etched the lines of her face, throwing into relief the up-

1

turned nose and sweet lips that were perhaps her greatest charm. Iva was very lovely and had undoubtedly everything that the average girl desires. Still she couldn't sleep, despite the fact that she had no worries and nothing more important on her mind than what she would do tomorrow. But even that had been dismissed long ago as unimportant. Iva enjoyed everything and was quite fancy-free.

She lay quietly, looking at the star, fascinated by its light. It seemed to dwarf all the others nearby and to Iva was more prominent than the moon itself which at present was hidden from her gaze.

"I wonder," she thought idly, "if that star is like the earth. I wonder if there are people there. It would be interesting to know. I wonder—."

A strange lassitude began to creep over her. It became an effort for her to think. The Star seemed to be coming nearer and nearer. She tried to force her mind to obey her, but she could not. Her entire concentration was upon the light that was rapidly approaching. "It must be the end of the world," was her last conscious thought as she was enveloped in a blaze of light that closed in all about her. She could almost feel it encompassing her. Then there was a weird rushing noise—and she knew no more.

* * *

Suddenly Iva was conscious of being very cold. She reached down to pull up the quilt but her hand touched nothing that even faintly resembled a cover. She opened her eyes and sat up in astonishment at what she saw.

She was lying in a garden, but a strange garden, the grass, instead of being green, was a most heavenly shade of blue, and the flowers were all different tones of the same color. Even the trees were blue, but the trunks, twisted and gnarled, were of a deep bluish-purple. Both trees and flowers were unlike any she had ever seen before.

"It's Gershwin's 'Rhapsody In Blue' come to life," she thought and looked upward. "Now I know I'm dreaming," she cried in astonishment, for the sky was rose—a deep rose—and the few fleecy clouds that she could see were pale pink. "It is like the most beautiful sunset I have ever seen," she said softly. The sound of her own voice was reassuring. She resorted to the old expedient of pinching herself and when it hurt she struggled to her feet. "I'm not dreaming, but this can't be real!"

Dimly she began to remember the star, the blaze of light, her own unconsciousness. "Perhaps I'm dead and this is Heaven," she remarked and began to walk along a path that was covered with blue gravel. Curiously she leaned over to pick up a piece of it. Then she gasped, for it was a sapphire she held in her two fingers, a stone far larger than any she had ever seen. The whole path was paved with such stones. As far as her eyes could reach, it wound along through the garden. She let the jewel slip through her fingers and walked on timidly. The path must lead somewhere and the Garden must have an owner.

The scent from the flowers was lovely, unlike anything she had ever smelt before. It was as though all the perfumes of the world had been concentrated into one essence. But there was no variation. All the flowers smelled alike. There was no sign of any birds or insects. Much as she hated such things, Iva would have welcomed the sight of a spider as some evidence that she was not the only living thing in a garden that so far as she could see, stretched for miles.

The air was mild, but as she had on only a thin nightgown of crepe de chine, she felt cold. The stones hurt her bare feet, so she walked on the grass alongside the path.

The flowers were arranged in beds with fanciful designs of which Iva could make nothing. The whole effect was rather futuristic.

Presently she came to a bubbling stream which wound in and out among the flowers. Its waters were crystal-clear, but they also were blue, of a shade so pale that it almost looked natural to Iva. She looked longingly at the water and for a moment hesitated as to whether she would dare to drink. Then she shrugged her shoulders and knelt down, making a cup of her hands.

"If I am dead, it can't hurt me; and if I'm in some strange place all alone, I'd be better dead. So here goes!" The water was deliciously cool and refreshing. It had no bad effects. Iva drank her fill and then arose to start on her pilgrimage into the unknown.

It seemed especially strange to Iva that there was no sign of life in the stream—no little minnows or other fish swimming about—only the clear water bubbling over deep-blue stones. The stones sparkled in the light from the Crimson Sun which had arisen since Iva first woke up. She had no doubt that the stones were sapphires too. The sun rays were warm, and Iva was grateful. For the first time she regretted that her hair was short.

All this time she had been unconsciously going up a slight. incline, and quite suddenly she arrived at the top of a little hill, from which she could see miles of the surrounding country.

In the distance she perceived a long, low, rambling building which had a tower at each corner of it, making four in all. From the tops of the towers a blue light radiated across the rose sky. The effect was very beautiful but Iva had reached the state where she was beyond the thought of beauty. The discovery of the building filled her with two sensations: relief that there must be human life of some kind or there would be no necessity for habitation, and ter- ror as to what the people might be like. Suppose she had gotten into a land of fantastic monsters or ghoulish figures. At any rate, they must have some kind of culture, for the land between the building and the hill on which she stood was wonderfully cultivated. The succession of trees, lagoons, waterways and flowers, except for the strangeness of their color and vegetation, all reminded Iva of the Gardens of Versailles; and the building itself, except for the tow- ers, was not unlike the palace Louis had built. From now on the ground was level, so Iva started towards the building, after she had rested awhile and surveyed the lovely landscape before her.

Iva's Puritan ancestry was standing her in good stead. Her fore- bears had been among that little band who left the mother-country England in the Mayflower to people a new land.

Iva, despite the strange thing that had happened to her, did not despair. She took a remarkably fatalistic view of things. If she had experienced death, she was to all intents and purposes still alive, and the process of dying was not as unpleasant as she had thought. If she had been wafted to some new land by as yet undiscovered means, she would make the best of it. She only hoped there would be something to make the best of, for she was growing hungry.

All at once she was struck by a new thought. Suppose she had walked in her sleep and perhaps something had happened to her eyes and destroyed her sense of color and made her see things as they were not. She ran lightly to the stream and used it as a mirror. Her own image stared back at her. Through the faint blue she could distinguish her flesh tints, the gold of her hair and the peach of her nightgown. Despite the rosy tint from the sun, her own colors held. Nothing was wrong with her eyes. In some strange way she had been transported to a Blue-Land.

Chapter II
The Palace of the Towers

As she had grown tired walking and her feet, unaccustomed to no protection, were sore, Iva sat by the edge of the stream and bathed them in the cool water.

"If I had something to eat and a coat, I'd be quite comfortable," she thought. Just then she heard the sound of a horn. She sprang to her feet and faced the direction the silvery notes had come from. Galloping over the blue grass was a group of horses with human beings on their backs.

Iva breathed a sigh of relief. At least, part of her suspense was over. Surely these people were men.

As they drew nearer, she began to distinguish them more plainly. The horses were very large but finely bred. They were like Arab steeds the size of Belgian truck horses. A deep purplish blue in color, their long manes and tails were of a periwinkle shade.

These details Iva took in quickly before she could see what the riders were like, but as they came nearer she could easily distinguish they were ridden by men—men with a pale bluish tinge to their skin. They had red hair which they wore long to their shoulders and were apparently naked save for a garment of some blue stuff about their hips, in the style of the Indian loin-cloth, which was held by a broad blue belt studded with sapphires. Iva gathered all this long before she glimpsed their features.

Eventually they came quite near and Iva counted ten men. They were very large men, at least six feet six, and they rode their horses as though part of them. In fact, Iva could see no harness and afterward discovered that they had neither reins nor saddles. Their features were clear-cut and somewhat aquiline. In their center was quite the best-looking man Iva ever had seen.

Tall and straight, perhaps half a head taller than the rest, he seemed to command. Around his forehead was a jeweled band made of the same material as the belts, in the center of which was a large blue stone which Iva was sure was a sapphire. His hair was a dark Titian shade of red and the blue tinge very faint on his skin. His nose was straight, his lips finely moulded. While his dark blue eyes breathed fire and spirit under his straight brows, still there was a kindliness in them.

They came very near to Iva and then stopped their horses, abruptly. The man with the band about his forehead directly faced Iva. He raised his right arm in salutation.

Iva responded by raising her right arm also.

A low murmur of awe swept through the men. Only the leader remained apparently unmoved.

Iva quickly lowered her arm. Then she looked into the man's face and smiled.

His eyes answered her but his lips didn't move. Finally he spoke in a strange language that she could make nothing of, but she was enchanted by the timbre of his voice, which was low and musical. Surely a man must be fine and cultured to have such a voice.

Iva shook her head. "I do not understand you," she said slowly, hoping perhaps he might know what she said. The hope was vain. He too shook his head sadly. Then he turned and spoke to his men. They rode about until they formed a circle around him and Iva. Only then did he descend from his horse, with a low whispered word to the great creature which stood silently where he left it.

The man came to Iva and struck his chest with his hands. "Ota," he cried.

Iva looked puzzled. He then pointed to one man after another and spoke a name, "Lotha—Gotha—Northa—Bulta—Mora—Noa—Legieta—Snowa—Tora," he said slowly, then again touched his chest and cried, "Ota!" as he looked questioningly at Iva.

Quite obviously he was telling her their names and desiring to know hers. She touched herself repeating "Iva" several times.

7

The man Ota seemed pleased. He repeated it to his followers who shouted it out in chorus. Iva noted that their voices were melodious too, but not as beautiful as that of the man called Ota. He seemed to excel in all things. She suspected that he must be a ruler, from the band about his head. She could now see that on the right side of the band was a yellow stone, one of green on the left, and when he turned his head she saw a great ruby in the back. Between these huge stones were innumerable smaller sapphires.

When the sound of their voices echoing her name had died away, Iva waited for the next move. It came quickly. A smile overspread Ota's face as he looked deep into her eyes. He gently patted her cheek and then picked her up in his arms.

At a low word his horse knelt down and Ota mounted, holding Iva very much as though she were a baby. Then as he spoke another word the horse rose slowly and gracefully. Iva marvelled at the sense of balance Ota possessed. She wondered still more during the swift ride to the building she had seen far away.

They must have covered sixty miles in an hour. Never had Iva believed horses could be capable of such speed. They fairly flew over the ground and were directed solely by words from their riders. Apparently they understood everything that was said to them.

Iva soon realized that she never would have been able to reach the Palace of the Towers by herself. They rode through miles and miles of the beautiful country she had seen from her hilltop.

Ota held her tightly against his breast. She could feel his heart beat as her head rested upon it. His arms were firm but tender. Occasionally he smiled down at her and eventually Iva's tired eyes closed. She was mentally and physically exhausted, but a sense of peace pervaded her. Ota seemed kindly and she felt she could trust him. It was entirely an innate sense that told her he was her friend. To be sure, he might be taking her to torture or death, but she did not think so. For the moment at least, in his arms, she felt safe, so she relaxed and went to sleep.

* * *

She did not awake until she heard the note of the horn again. Then she woke up, instantly remembering all that had happened.

They were in front of the building with the four towers. Tall and far apart, the towers were sharply etched upon the crimson sky. The building near to looked more like Versailles than ever, only that it was twice as big and of a peculiar shade of blue that Iva could find no comparison for.

She moved a little and raised her head for a better view but Ota pressed her back against him. Putting his mouth close to her ear, he whispered, "Ssh," in the language universal. She knew he meant her to be silent. So she was, but she watched proceedings with a great deal of interest.

They were in front of huge gates with lodge houses on either side. From these houses issued a score of men. They were clad in the same loincloths that her captors wore, only they were scantier and the material was a different shade of blue. Their belts had no jewels in them save one sapphire near the buckle. These men, some hundred or more, swung open the gates at a word from Ota and at another command someone brought a blue blanket which Ota put around Iva, covering all of her except her eyes.

They swept through the gates and on towards the Palace, up an avenue lined on either side with enormous towering trees which were absolutely uniform in size, shape and color.

Eventually they drew up alongside of a long flight of blue marble steps. One of the other men lifted her down, and held her while Ota dismounted.

For the first time Iva felt a twinge of fear, but when Ota took her back again it disappeared. He strode rapidly up the steps followed by the nine men. They passed many guards stationed at various intervals, before they entered the Palace. Each guard saluted Ota who inclined his head in answer.

They went through various halls, into a great room which seemed to take in a huge amount of space. Many columns supported the ceiling, and upper floors Iva supposed. At the far end was a throne on a raised dais, which was empty. The entire room was deserted except for rows of guards who lined the walls.

They passed through the Throne Room, as Iva christened it, without stopping, and through several rooms beyond it which she was too tired to notice. Then they climbed another stairway and finally came to a halt in a large, square room which was furnished with low couches piled high with cushions. One whole side of the wall was made of some transparent material which permitted a gorgeous view of the Gardens surrounding the Palace for vast distances.

Ota spoke rapidly to his friends. They all raised their right hands at the end of his words and spoke together in unison. Then they left the room. Iva and Ota were alone.

Reluctantly he put her on her feet. Iva pulled the blanket close about her, realizing how scantily she was clad. This Ota did not like. He shook his head and pulled it away from her, and flung it on the nearest couch.

For the first time Iva felt fear. After all she was alone and this was a man, with all a man's desires, apparently, from the look in his eyes. She drew back a step, but swiftly he was on his knees in front of her, his hands upraised pleadingly.

Iva did not know what he wanted but a sudden wave of pity for his inarticulateness swept over her. She smiled and put her hand on his shoulder.

With a little gasp of joyousness, Ota caught her in his arms.

Iva was afraid but she did not find his touch unpleasant. For a few seconds they remained so, then Ota sprang to his feet and moved several paces away from her. In a little while she heard footsteps and realized he had heard them long before she had.

In a few minutes more a small, wizened old woman entered the room escorted by the man Ota had designated as Noa. The old woman was naked as the men. She wore a many-colored blue scarf draped about her hips, fastened with a belt, similar to the men's only hers was narrower.

The three conversed several minutes together, Ota apparently urging some course neither the old woman nor Noa approved of. At length Ota snapped out a sharp command and the others bowed low. Noa clapped his hands, at which a man brought in a tray with a flask of some blue liquid and two glasses upon it, laid it on one of the couches and departed silently.

The woman reached into a bag she wore suspended from her belt and extracted a small pellet. Noa poured out a glass full of the liquid. The woman dropped the pellet into it; then she advanced towards Iva.

Iva, sensing that she was to drink the mixture, shrank back. Ota, who was watching her narrowly, took the goblet from the woman and raised it to his lips, swallowing a little to show her that it was quite safe. But then, instead of giving it to her, he handed it to Noa and went to a low chest in a far corner of the room. He opened it, leaned down and came back with something in his hand. He came close to Iva and she saw that he carried a headband similar to his own—and a belt. Both were beautifully studded with sapphires. The old woman cried out something and dropped on her knees before Ota, but he only shook his head.

Noa protested too. Iva could tell from his tone that he was begging Ota to change his mind, but his pleas had no effect.

Calmly Ota bound the belt about Iva's waist, put the jeweled band about her head so that the great sapphire it contained was in the middle of her forehead, and then he leaned over and kissed her gently on the mouth.

Iva, not knowing what the ceremony meant but sensing it was for her protection, touched the belt and band with her two hands simultaneously, then bowed low to Ota and extended her hand to him. He clasped it firmly in his own and turned to the others with a pleased expression, which did not change before the worried look on their faces.

Still holding her right hand, he reached for the goblet with his left and handed it to Iva. She took it and raising it as though she were toasting him, she drank it down. At that moment she would have done anything Ota asked; besides, she was faint for lack of food.

The liquid tasted like a strong wine. It burned her throat. She could feel its fire inside her. But a weird, drowsy feeling came in its wake. She swayed slightly. Was it the end, she wondered! Had Ota betrayed her after all, this man whom already she had learned to love?

For the second time in her life she could no longer concentrate her thoughts. She was growing numb and her feet could not hold her. She became absolutely limp and would have fallen, only Ota caught her in his arms. As he carried her towards the couch, she heard Noa say, "Without doubt this is one the Great Mind called from another world," and then she drifted into slumber without wondering how she could have understood the strange new language.

Chapter III
The Round Room

Iva awoke to find herself surrounded by a group of women. There must have been thirty at least and they all seemed to be young. They were clad only in the piece of silk wrapped around their hips. Their breasts were very small and undeveloped. They could have passed almost for boys, except for the feminine contour of their faces and hips. They were quite pretty with bluish skin and eyes and flaming red hair.

The girls were pointing at Iva, making signs to one another, but they spoke no word. They seemed full of curiosity and one or two even ventured to touch the silk of Iva's gown. When Iva sat up they drew back a few paces, then simultaneously they all knelt before her.

Iva swung herself around so that her feet touched the floor. Then she motioned for them to arise. They obeyed her and stood silently.

"Where is—" began Iva, and then stopped, realizing the hopelessness of trying to make them understand her desire to know where Ota was. She repeated his name several times, hoping they would comprehend. One of the prettiest of the girls came forward and kneeling in front of Iva, opened her mouth wide indicating that Iva should look.

Iva leaned over and peered into the girl's mouth. She drew back in horror for the girl had no tongue. The girl made an encompassing gesture which took in all the others. Then she laid her head on Iva's knee and kissed Iva's hand.

Iva patted the bowed crimson curls while hot tears welled up in her eyes. Was this the fate of all the girls in this strange land into which she had been strangely transported? Would it be hers? She comforted herself with the thought of the old woman. She had had a tongue and had not hesitated to use it. Iva wondered why they had not wanted Ota to give her the belt. Ota! Already her heart beat faster at the thought of his coming.

Would he be as she remembered him? Would she still feel towards him as she had last night? That is, she supposed it was last night, for the red sun was still shining in the rosy sky. She could hardly bear the suspense. Would he be kind to her? The memory of his kiss swept over her, and she felt the color rush to her face.

Men had never meant very much in Iva's life. She had held herself aloof from them and their casual caresses, because she had never met the one to whom she could respond.

But here in the midst of this terrifying adventure that had come to her, she had found a man for whom she could care, whose touch had awakened emotions within her that she had never dreamed she possessed. And the man who had brought love to life in the depths of her being was someone of whom she knew nothing. He might be married or a cannibal or all sorts of more frightful things than she could possibly bear to conceive even in her thoughts. She could hardly stand the suspense of not knowing how he would treat her now. Again she cried, "Ota!" and pointed to the door.

The girl smiled and nodded. Then she pulled Iva gently to her feet. One of the other girls brought forward a length of silk. The girl made motion to Iva to remove her night-gown. Iva demurred and the girl held up the piece of silk for her inspection.

It was beautifully woven of a periwinkle blue with a design of flowers in a deeper shade. The girl pointed to her own more simple band and then wrapt the other around Iva in dumb show. Then again, having removed it, she motioned Iva to take off her gown.

Iva was afraid refusal might make them unpleasant, so she started to unfasten the belt Ota had given her. The women shivered as her fingers touched the buckle. The girl quickly restrained Iva and began to pull her gown. As the belt was not very tight, it came through easily enough. Presently the gown was drawn over her head and Iva stood with no other covering than the belt in the center of the thirty women. They made funny little sounds which Iva took to be admiration from their expression.

The girl laid her own arm next to Iva's and pointed to the difference in its color. Side by side it was really amazing. Iva's pink skin intensified the blueish tinge of the other.

When they had done admiring her, they bathed her with towels dipped in water, and dried her with others that had been perfumed with the scent of the flowers she had smelt before. Then the girl wrapped the silk around Iva; beginning in the front it passed around her body several times and finally each end—that is where they had begun to wind it and where they finished was drawn up under the belt, being passed under and over it several times so that it was quite secure.

Iva walked over to the side of the room that was transparent. She had supposed last night that it was a wall of glass, but she was wrong. It was a thick substance, perfectly translucent, clearer than any glass Iva had ever seen. There was no opening in it, nor any window in the room, yet the air was pure—why or how Iva did not know. She looked out at the Gardens. Here and there she saw guards posted, but there was no other sign of life. She put her hand on the transparent wall but it was solid and cold and did not give to her touch.

The girl plucked at her arm, and when Iva turned led her to the other side of the room where two of the women held a huge polished shield made of some shiny blue metal. The girl piloted her in front of it and then stepped back, clapping her hands.

It was a crude mirror, but Iva was not displeased with the picture it contained. The barbaric dress—or lack of dress—was becoming, she decided as she looked. The band about her forehead with the great sapphire in its center, proved a marvelous foil for her golden curls.

Iva breathed a silent prayer of thanksgiving that she had a good figure and her hair was naturally curly. She smiled at the women, and the girl brought her back to the couch, heaping many pillows behind her.

Iva settled back comfortably. One of the little band picked up a queer looking instrument, somewhat like a small harp, and began drawing melody from its strings—strange, sweet strains unlike any music Iva had ever heard, and infinitely more beautiful. The other women lay about on the floor, the girl sitting at Iva's feet.

The scene was strange, barbaric, and somehow seemed unreal to Iva. Here she was, a perfectly normal girl, suddenly in surroundings such as had never been. These queer blue people with their red hair were fantastic. Even Ota, though her pulse quickened at his name, was unreal. What would her friends say if they could see her as she was now, or her family?

Till this moment Iva had been too occupied with a strange land, people and happenings, to think of her home. Even now she didn't dare dwell too much on her mother and father. If she were dead, they would be mourning for her. But at least she would see them again when they too—but if not, she didn't know. In her mind she could not venture a guess as to what the other possibilities might be; they were beyond imagining.

From somewhere a gong struck. Its reverberations echoed through the Palace. The girl at Iva's feet sprang up and taking Iva's hand pulled her gently up.

"Ota?" asked Iva.

The girl nodded and led Iva through the heavily carved door, which was opened by two guards, out into a long corridor. It seemed to Iva that they walked miles, at intervals passing guards who saluted them. Eventually they reached a tiny jewel-studded door. The girl showed some emblem to the man who guarded it. He then knocked twice, pressed the surface with his hand and presently as the door swung open, they passed through.

On the other side was an entrance hall, then three large rooms through which they passed. In the last the girl pressed a panel in the wall which swung back revealing a flight of steps which they descended.

The door swung to behind them leaving no trace of its existence. Then another long passage, only this was very narrow and dark and had no guards.

After many twists and turns, they came to another tiny door. That is, it was an ordinary sized door to Iva, but small for these tall people who had to stoop to pass through. The girl took a small key from her belt and rapped sharply on the door, then inserted the key. Iva could see no lock, but when the girl turned the key the door swung inwards.

The girl kept the key and motioned to Iva to go ahead. Iva passed through. The door swung shut behind her, but not before Iva noticed that the girl had thrown herself down on the floor on the other side of the door.

No sound was heard as the door closed. Iva stepped forward and found herself in a perfectly round room with a very high ceiling that went up into a point and looked very much like the inside of an opened umbrella, the rafters taking the place of the ribs. From them were suspended hundreds of belts. Later Iva noticed that they were of four colors, blue, red, green and yellow, some studded elaborately with jewels of the corresponding shades, some almost plain. But at the moment Iva saw nothing but Ota who stood gravely regarding her. Behind him was a couch heaped with cushions which, except for a small chest, constituted the only furniture.

Iva smiled at him uncertainly.

He began to speak in his own soft musical language which, strangely enough, Iva understood.

"So, I see you dressed as the women of my country. You are more beautiful than I dreamed possible."

Bewildered, Iva tried to answer, and to her even greater astonishment found she could put her words into his language. "How do I understand what you say? Where am I?"

Ota held out his hand. Unhesitatingly, Iva gave him hers. "I will tell you everything which you desire to know, and explain all things to you, but it will take time. You must be comfortable. Come, lie here." He guided her to the couch and fixed the pillows for her at one end, reluctantly relinquishing her hand.

When she was quite settled, he established himself on the couch facing her, cross-legged, in Oriental fashion. "Later I will say what is in my heart, but now I will satisfy your curiosity. You understand my language and are able to speak it because I had the tablet of wisdom given to you. In our country it is given to each child at the age of five and then they speak and understand. At intervals they are given more tablets and learn other things, until at the age of fifteen they have acquired all wisdom. You were only given the language tablet. Later if you like you shall have the others, but for you it must be slower, for you are not a child. Now you both understand and can speak my tongue. But by my belt, I beg you to speak it only to me."

Iva laughed, a tinkly little giggle that echoed through the room.

"It is no laughing matter; when you know all the customs of my country you will understand better." Ota spoke gravely.

Suddenly serious, Iva swung about so that she, too, sat curled up upon her feet, facing him directly instead of sideways. "I want to know all your customs, but most of all I want to know what your country is. Where am I?"

The man looked over at the fair young girl who faced him so bravely and pity was in his eyes as he spoke, "You are in the Country of Ota." Then after a short silence, he explained, "Which is on Venus."

Chapter IV
Iva Learns Many Things

"The planet Venus!" Iva almost gasped with astonishment. She was not dead. She was still alive but had been transported from Earth to Venus. She had never even thought that she was not on her own planet. It seemed to her she might have guessed.

She remembered reading a book by someone named Burroughs about a man who had been transported to Mars. Now she had reached Venus by some strange agency. Perhaps some day a book would be written about her. "Venusian Adventures." Perhaps her mother might read it, her mother whom she would never see again. Hot tears welled up in her eyes and down her cheeks at the thought.

Ota put his hand on hers, "Don't, Earth-child. I will make you happy!"

She looked up at him and read the love and pity in his eyes and her heart missed a beat. Her fingers clung to his while she wiped away the tears with her free hand. Iva was one of those rare people who can cry and still look beautiful.

"I wish I had a vessel to catch the liquid from your eyes. It is precious. Here we never do what you are doing, not even if we lose our belts."

Iva controlled herself. "How did I get here?"

"The Great Mind called you!" he said.

"The Great Mind?" Iva questioned.

Ota moved nearer and still holding her hand clasped in his began: "The Great Mind is our ruler. In order to make you understand, I must explain to you about this planet.

"Venus is divided into four great countries or lands; the Blue Land, which is Ota's; the Red Land, which is Leta's; the Yellow Land of Toa's and the Green Land which is ruled by Pra. We four rule absolutely in our own kingdoms. We never interfere with each other. We dare not, for there is a law if one Venusian attack another Venusian, the other two colors must help the one attacked. So war amongst us four is impossible. We each have many peoples and tribes in our own land, some of which we have never seen even ourselves, there are so many unexplored parts of Venus."

"But who," interrupted Iva, "is the Great Mind? One of you rulers?"

Ota shook his head. "In the very center of our Planet is a huge area of land, a fan-shaped piece taken from each country, which forms an immense circle. A Golden Palace stands directly in the centre of this land, in which lives the Great Mind. He rules the entire planet. His word is law to Leta, Toa, Pra, and myself."

"Is he a god?" Iva's eyes were wide with astonishment over this revelation.

"His word is absolute. All of us Venusians worship him. He alone has the power of the belt."

"Whatever is that?"

"Each of us is given at birth a belt. It grows as we do and is never removed. Without it we could not exist. If it is taken from us, we perish, sometimes quickly, sometimes slowly, but always life goes from us as we age into nothingness if we lose our belts. The Great Mind is the only one who has power to order the removal of anyone's belt. If someone commits a grave or heinous crime, he or she is taken to the Great Mind after the trial, and he makes the final decision. If his word is that the unfortunate must lose his or her belt, it is removed with great ceremony and given to the person sinned against. Then the guilty one is cast forth. No one may befriend such a one. Soon the body weakens and becomes inanimate. It is then thrown into a fiery pit and burned."

Iva's hand clutched Ota's more firmly. "You mean, if I took this off I should die?" She gently touched the belt she wore. Now she understood why the women were so horrified when she had started to unbuckle it.

Ota looked puzzled. "I do not know what you mean by 'die'. If you had no belt, you would become inanimate, your body would age and being useless would be burnt."

"That is what we on earth call death. It is when the spirit leaves the body. It happens to all of us," Iva tried to explain, though she spoke haltingly, groping for the new words like a baby just learning to talk.

"How sad!" cried Ota. "Here—no one—what do you call it?"

"Dies," Iva supplied the word.

Ota went on, "No one dies, unless they lose their belt by decree of the Great Mind. Once in my own household it happened that a girl was accused of burning a rival so badly that the skin could not heal, which with us is rare. She was tried and condemned, and the Great Mind had her belt taken from her. Later I found the girl was not guilty. A spurned lover had done the deed, leaving false clues pointing to the girl for revenge. I sent out men to find her. They did, almost on the edge of the Green Land. She was very weak. A little longer and she would have been inanimate; but they brought her here in time, even before she had begun to age. I gave her a belt and she revived. When I made my yearly pilgrimage to the Great Mind, I told him this and he forgave my usurping his prerogative and confirmed the girl in her possession of the belt. She is devoted to me now and full of gratitude. Her name is Erda and it is she who brought you here, for I trust her absolutely with all my secrets."

"I like her too. She was sweet to me but she has no tongue so we could not speak, though then I did not know I would understand."

"She comes from a people who have no tongues. They live in a far wild corner of my country. We often raid their land, for they make good slaves when they are tamed."

"Where do the belts come from?" Iva was tremendously interested in the belts, now that she possessed one.

"They are woven by Virgins of each land of some especially grown fiber which is sent us by the Great Mind. Then they are taken to him and infused with magic powers. What more would you know, most beautiful?"

"There is so much I want to hear, so many questions to be answered, I hardly know where to begin. You never take off your belts, not even when you bathe?"

A slow smile passed over Ota's finely moulded lips. "It is not necessary. They do not get wet, nor do they wear out. They are Eternal as we are. They are never removed save as punishment, except in one instance. When a man takes a maid to wife, he takes off her belt and replaces it instantly with one of his house, the arrangement and color of the jewels being symbols."

Iva felt his eyes piercing hers. Again swift color stained her cheeks.

The man went on, "The ceremony of the belt is our marriage service. In the case of a ruler, a forehead band is also given."

"But then, according to that," stammered Iva, "I—I am your wife."

Ota rose leisurely and his great form towered above Iva for a moment. Then quite suddenly he was on his knees before her.

"Ota," he said, and the low musical tones of his voice thrilled Iva to the depths of her being, "Ota pays homage to Iva, his wife, Lady of the Blue Land."

Chapter V
The Story of Ula

For several moments there was silence in the Round Room. Then Iva smiled, a little, soft tremulous curving of her lips. Ota held out his arms and she leaned towards him. Their lips met. He kissed her as a man kisses the woman he loves, and Iva responded. He held her closely in his arms and for a little while time was forgotten.

"Ia dowa sea," he whispered over and over again, and Iva knew it meant "I love you," and cried it back to him out of the depths of her heart.

All the terror and strangeness were gone; even the longing for her dear ones whom she would never see again was swept away by the joy of being in this man's arms and hearing him say the magic words, "I love you."

Presently Ota released her. "Even here this is madness. We set in motion currents we know nothing of that may reach the Great Mind even from this magic chamber. My Lady and my Wife, make yourself comfortable again. There is still much that you must know."

Iva obediently curled up upon the divan and Ota resumed his position facing her.

"There is so much to tell you, but perhaps I had better begin at the beginning."

"How I came here?" she suggested.

The man shook his head. "In order to make that clear to you, I must go farther back—even to the beginning of my life which was thousands of aeons ago."

It seemed incredulous to Iva that the man she was looking at and whom she loved was older than she could possibly comprehend. He looked to be about thirty, in the fullest development of his manhood. It was almost impossible for Iva to realize how wise he must be She forced speculation from her mind to listen to his words.

"Once the Blue Land was ruled over by Ula, who was a great man and a great ruler, but he grew too powerful to suit the Great Mind who would brook no one's interference. Now, Ula studied ancient books which he found buried in ruins from the age before ours, and he grew wise in magic, and he had this room built for himself by slaves, but when it was completed he took their belts from them, locking them up here until they died, as you call it. Then in great secrecy he had them burnt. There was no one to tell the tale of the Round Room which he had hidden in the depths of his Palace. He had bound it so about with his magic that not even the Great Mind's power could pierce its walls. Here he was quite safe. Then he hung the belts of the slaves he had exterminated from the rafters, put his books behind those panels—" Ota indicated the carved wooden walls, "and came here often to study and grow great so that he could some day overthrow the Great Mind and the rulers of the other lands and unite the whole of Venus under him. It was a stupendous plot."

Iva nodded breathlessly. She was entirely absorbed in the tale she was hearing.

With a smile for her, Ota went on, "When I tell you that the Great Mind knows all things, that nothing except what happens in this little room can be hidden from him, you will realize how much Ula was undertaking. He had to keep all thoughts of such things and even his new wisdom from his thoughts when he was about so the Great Mind could not guess. But he did it. The Great Mind knew nothing of Ula's plot to usurp the Golden Throne, but some stray thoughts that Ula could not keep in check, the Great Mind drew to himself and knew that there must be more behind. The Great Mind tried to trap Ula but Ula was too quick for him, for he had grown almost as wise in magic as the Great Mind himself; so the Great Mind had to devise another scheme. Now I make my entrance into the story."

"I have been waiting for your name," cried Iva.

Ota continued, "I was a son of the Great Mind's by one of his concubines. You must know that he never takes a wife, for there is in all Venus no one fit to share his throne. But he has many slave-girls. Strangely enough in all the aeons but one of them has ever produced a child. The Great Mind is so mental that the physical is not strong in him. Nevertheless, I was born and as his only child, had great honor in the Golden City.

"One day my Father sent for me and told me of Ula and what he knew. 'A test of your wisdom, my son,' he cried. 'What can we do to trap the ruler of the Blue Land and take his belt from him?'

"I thought a little while and then I answered, 'Sometimes a woman's kiss weakens the strongest mind'."

"My Father clapped his hands. 'Of a truth, you are my son! So I had decided. I but sent for you to test your wisdom and to ask you which of the maidens seemed best suited for the purpose.'

"I sent my thoughts over all the slaves of my Father, the Great Mind, and finally said, 'Efa is the most beautiful.'

"Efa was sent for and truly she was lovely according to our standards, who had never seen beauty such as yours, my Lady."

Iva smiled at the compliment, but was silent. She did not want to interrupt the thread of his story.

Ota continued, "Efa was well instructed in what she must do and agreed to everything. In fact she was most appreciative of the honor. So one night she was left in Ula's gardens near the Palace. I was in command of the band that conducted her from the Golden City. Before we galloped back we took her belt from her.

"Alone, she struggled to Ula's door. His guards brought her to him and she told a well-wrought tale of having been condemned by the Great Mind to lose her belt. She cursed the Great Mind, and Ula was amazed at her daring. 'It is well for you the Great Mind sleeps while you speak,' he told her.

"Efa laughed. 'The Great Mind has forgotten already the slave who displeased him, but you, my Lord, are kind. Give me a belt, and let me live to serve you.'

"She was beautiful and Ula loved beauty. Moreover he had not taken a new slave for many moons, being immersed in his studies. All at once his passions welled up within him. 'So be it,' he said and he took a belt and fastened it about her waist.

"I must explain to you," Ota broke into his narrative, "that each ruler has a supply of belts given by the Great Mind to be used for his household. For instance, the belt you wear was given to me when I first received my own for the day when I should take a wife. Then the belt that she had had I would keep and eventually return to the Hall of Belts in the Golden City. Likewise I have other belts with my symbols for new slaves, but they are all accounted for and numbered in the Hall of Belts and report is made of them to the Great Mind."

"I understand," said Iva.

"Ula became like one mad over Efa. He hardly left her side and for a little while forgot his plans. Efa, too, forgot her part and returned his love. For awhile they were very happy. I begged my Father to recall Efa, but the Great Mind said, 'Wait,' so we did, and as he had foreseen, Ula's passion spent itself. Ula began to leave Efa for hours upon hours. Then day after day she did not see him. Efa was as one possessed. She was not working for the Great Mind but for herself. She was fighting for her love. With every wile woman knows she tried to find out what took him from her. Finally she succeeded. To prove his love for her in a moment of passion and madness, Ula told his plot to seize the Golden City. It was all the Great Mind needed. He could not read Ula's thoughts, but Efa's were open to him despite her efforts to close them. He sent me to summon Ula to the Golden City on pretense of having learned he had given Efa a belt.

"Ula came quite unsuspecting, for even his magic had not yet reached the point of reading men's thoughts, save in a small way. Another aeon and he had been my Father's equal.

"As it was, he confessed to giving Efa the belt and begged for confirmation of this, 'For,' he said, 'I love her and would make her my wife.'

"The Great Mind laughed and his laughter filled the Great Hall of the Golden Palace. 'So some day you could share my throne with her?' he asked.

"Ula stepped back in horror that the Great Mind knew his plan, and looked reproachfully at Efa.

"My Father spoke again, 'You shall lose your belt and while you are becoming inanimate you shall be tortured unless you tell the source of your wisdom.'

"For not even to Efa had Ula mentioned the Round Room he had built, nor the ancient writings he had discovered.

"Ula said nothing, but in view of all the assemblage he undid his belt and took off his head-band. He laid them both at the Great Mind's feet.

"My Father turned to Efa, 'You would not have told me Ula's secret of your own accord; yet because you have helped me you shall not lose your belt, but you shall be punished because you tried to keep Ula's plot from me. Your belt shall be taken from you at regular intervals until you have aged and lost your beauty. Then you can have it for all time again. An old woman in a Land of Youth, that is punishment enough.'

"Ula, who had asked no mercy for himself, begged it for her, for the doom the Great Mind had spoken is considered even worse than annihilation by us and is meted out very rarely. However, my Father was adamant. Efa was led away to have the sentence executed, and before Ula had become inanimate, she was old and wrinkled.

"Then the torturing of Ula commenced, for he refused to speak. Our bodies are impervious to anything but fire, so while he aged and began to become inanimate, they burned his skin deeply to the bone. But even then his mind was impenetrable and finally he became shriveled and inanimate, and his body was burned without our having learned the source of his wisdom.

"Then the Great Mind called a concourse in the Hall of the Golden Palace and before all put Ula's belt and forehood hand upon me, proclaiming me the Ruler of Ula's Country."

Chapter VI
The Son of the Great Mind

"Before I left to take up my abode in this, the Palace of the Four Towers, which Ula had built for a country residence, I had one last interview with my Father.

"'Son of my body,' he told me, 'I have raised you to great heights but always remember I can as easily bring you down from them as I put you up. You have all power over the Blue Land, but to me you are subservient. In Ula's Palace perhaps you can discover Ula's secrets. If you do, lose no time in telling me and by our mental communication I will tell you what to do. In order to make it easy for you to speak with me through your mind, I give you the word of communion. You have but to speak it and instantly our thoughts will interchange.'

"The Great Mind whispered to me the word so powerful that even here in this magic chamber I dare not think it. Then he sent for Efa and told me I should take her with me, for perhaps she might be useful to me.

"When Efa was led in, I drew back in horror. The last time I had seen her she had been beautiful, now she was an old and wrinkled hag. My Father took no notice of the change, but he spoke kindly to her. 'Do you swear by your belt, allegiance to my son?'

"She knelt before me and kissed my hand and belt in token of her submission. Since then she has been always with me. It was Efa who gave you the drink that made you understand."

Iva nodded, "I wondered why she alone was old."

"Here and there one finds someone who has been so punished, otherwise we retain our youth forever."

Iva wondered why the Planet was not overcrowded and stored the question away for some future time. Just now she asked, "What happened then?"

With a toss of the reddish locks about his face, Ota replied, "My revulsion to Efa, who was the first old-looking person I had ever seen was, at that moment, great. I looked at her and thought that but for her beauty, which was now a thing of the past, Ula would still have been all-powerful, and I swore a mighty oath, 'Now, by the Red Sun and my Father, the Great Mind, I will not wed. No woman on all our Planet shall ever be my Lady and my Wife!'

"The Great Mind laughed and said, 'Like the Father the Son,' and bade me begone."

"We have a proverb like that in my own country," Iva interrupted.

"Perhaps all great truths are universal." I left that night and after many suns of travel reached my domain. The people all accepted me joyously, feeling that with the son of the Great Mind to guide them, all would be well for them. Ula's sons became my counselors and my friends. They were with me when I found you."

"Didn't they resent their Father's death?"

Ota shook his head. "Why should they? Here on Venus we are individuals. We love the women we choose for our wives, we love the men we choose for our comrades, but we do not love the people who call us in to being to gratify a passing passion unless it so happens that those persons endear themselves to us."

"What a simple arrangement," though Iva, "and how much trouble it would save on Earth. Still, for a mother not to love her child or a child not to care for its mother would seem strange. Half of the joy of life would be missing." Out loud she asked, "Don't you love your father and mother?"

The Ruler of the Blue Land laughed and the sound of his laughter was like deep chords on a harp. "To love the Great Mind were not possible. One feels not affection for an intellect, no matter how one might admire it, and as for my mother, I have seen her only twice in my life. When you understand how we are brought up you will comprehend, but now I must waste no more time. Your too long absence will be remarked. I must finish my tale and quickly."

"I won't interrupt again," Iva told him.

"I found no hint of any of Ula's secrets, neither did I find out anything from Efa. But I did win her devotion. I communicated this to the Great Mind and he dismissed the matter as settled.

"Then one day, quite by accident, I found the secret panel in my sleeping-chamber. I explored and discovered this room and the old manuscripts. They fascinated me. By the power that Ula's belt had gathered from his magics, I was able to read them.

"I spoke the word to tell my Father of my find, but the power of this room was stronger than that of the word and when I received no answer from the Great Mind, I realized what Ula had accomplished. Then I yielded to temptation. I was quite safe from discovery, as safe as Ula had been. I would imbibe his wisdom before I told my Father of my find. I might as well gain the knowledge of the ages that had gone before with their lost wisdom. So I did, entrusting my secret to none except Erda. I taught her to make her mind a blank, as Ula had done, which I had soon discovered, so my Father could learn nothing.

"So I have studied day after day, night after night, until I am more powerful than Ula ever was, and have twice the wisdom and lore of magic had by him. I alone on all Venus can stand against the Great Mind, and by my belt I trust that it is so!"

Despite herself Iva interrupted again, "But why should you want to fight your Father who has done so much for you?" she questioned, wonderingly.

The Ruler of the Blue Land let his eyes pass over Iva's slight form before he answered, "Because I love you I must battle with my Father, for the Great Mind wants you for himself."

Chapter VII
The Earth Girl

"**Y**ou mean your Father wants to marry me?" stammered Iva, aghast at this cloud in a sky that had heretofore been bright.

"Briefly I will tell you. Affairs on Venus have been quiet. There have been no petty wars, for the wild tribes have behaved well and paid their tributes. There have been no intrigues or great crimes for the past aeon, so the Great Mind grew restless for something to excite him. Women were brought to him from all over Venus, but they could no longer rouse his faded appetites. From sheer boredom the Great Mind sent his thoughts farther afield through the universe and once or twice he established a slight contact with Earth, enough at least to know that on that planet were women different from ours.

"For centuries he has been working to find a way to transport one hither alive. Several he drew a little way from the earth only to lose them. But at last he discovered how it could be done, and he called me to the speaking bowl and told me that at last he was successful in his research and ready to transport an Earth Girl to Venus for his pleasure."

Iva shivered a little. All at once she was terribly afraid.

The man sensed this. "Fear not, my love," he said. "Are you not Ota's wife? Think you he will not protect his own?"

"I know you will." Her shivering stopped.

"The Great Mind also told me that he had no idea just where on Venus the girl would find herself, but he was proclaiming throughout the entire planet his expectancy of an Earth Girl and that she was to be treated with all consideration and brought to him. Of course he would know when she appeared and would send further instructions to whoever found her.

"Yesterday," continued Ota, "I was restless all day. Strange forces seemed at work within me, so I called my friends together and we got ready to ride. Just before we left, I looked in my divining globe and I saw you lying in my Garden, asleep. At that moment Love entered my heart."

Iva bent down and softly kissed his hand.

"I knew at once you were the Earth Girl and that I must have you for my own. The fact that you were not of our Planet released me from my vow not to wed. I told my friends I had discovered you and together we rode to where you were."

"I was so afraid," Iva told him, "until I looked into your eyes, and then everything changed for me. It was what we call 'love at first sight'."

"Truly well named, and so were you. When I learned your name was Iva, my very inmost being rejoiced. All of our names end with 'a'. But there was another reason, as I shall tell you later. It seems strange that you should have been so called."

"My mother made it up out of her own head. She said that she wanted something different for me. She little knew—" Iva's voice broke.

"I have no doubt that she drew the name from one of the thought emanations of our Planet. Undoubtedly that is why you were successfully brought hither. There is great power in words, and your name being as ours was a link." Ota spoke half to himself.

There was another silence. Iva watched Ota's face. Despite the blue tinge of his skin she was quite sure that she had never seen a man on earth who was so handsome.

Finally Ota spoke again. "I brought you here and all the time we were riding I dreamed dreams, first being sure that I had bound my thoughts safely so my Father could not read them, as I have power to do. I even tried a new spell to safeguard the thoughts of my companions, which apparently worked well, for the Great Mind did not know you had been found. That is why I didn't let anyone see you as I brought you in.

"I bound my friends to silence and sent Noa for Efa. While we were alone I discovered you were not averse to me. I sensed that you returned my affection. Then I made Efa give you the pellet of Language against her will, for she knew that the Great Mind had issued no such order. Then to their utter horror, I gave you the belt and the hand that proclaimed you my Wife and Lady of the Blue Land.

"When the effects of the pellet sent you to sleep, I swore them to silence and bound their thoughts. Then I worked a most powerful spell and encompassed the whole Palace with a hand of such strength that no thought can pass through it unless I allow it or lift off the invisible cloud that protects everyone within these walls. That is why I could allow you to be seen.

"Here we are absolutely safe in my Round Room, and I think that unless the Great Mind can combat my magic, we are secure in the Palace. But now we must decide what our next move will be."

The girl from the earth looked at the Venus man. "It's so strange and wonderful that somehow I cannot take it all in. But I do understand, more or less, only, Ota," for the first time speaking his name in his presence, she lingered over it as though reluctant to have it finally leave her lips, "I cannot see why you should have loved me. It's too marvelous!"

"You were meant for me. In one of these books that Ula found is a prophecy made aeons and aeons ago. When I have taught you to decipher the writings, I will show it to you. It says, 'When the ruler, Ota, takes the girl Iva to be his wife, then is the time when all Venus shall be united and wax greater in power than ever before.' So—" Ota tossed the hair from his shoulders, "It was predestined we should be mated. Only, remember I loved you before I ever knew your name."

"That will always be a precious thought to me." As Iva put her thoughts into words of Ota's language, she unconsciously adopted the flowing phraseology that distinguished his speech. All the slang and colloquisms of the twentieth century seemed to have slipped away from her.

Ota spoke again, this time very seriously, "Now we must decide the course of our future actions. And one more thing you must know to help your decision. Immediately after the ceremony of the belt you were my Wife and First Lady of the Blue Land, but according to our laws you may not become so in actual fact until the passing of six red suns. At the end of that time I must bring you to the Temple and the High Priest of the Sun anoints you as a Virgin, if you were not when I took you to the Temple, they would refuse to recognize the marriage and you would be only a concubine—neither my Wife nor First Lady."

"How long is six Red Suns' passing?" stammered Iva, who was embarrassed at the frankness of his talk.

"Each sun stays with us six of your days and sets upon the seventh day during which it is entirely dark. It corresponds to your night. So the Great Mind told me who from his wisdom learned a little of your ways. That makes forty-two days that we must wait or as I call it, six suns. Yesterday was the first tala (or day) of the Red Sun, so one day is gone."

"So one day is gone," repeated Iva.

Ota continued, "I do not know if my spells are powerful enough to hold that long or whether the Great Mind will be able to work a counter magic. I think I can trust all my people, but the Great Mind may have a spy in my Palace. I am not even sure whether he knows if you reached Venus or not. I dare not send my thought to find out.

"If he does not know that you are here, and his thoughts may have been busy elsewhere at the time of your arrival, I can tell him his experiment was not a success, and perhaps keep your presence here secret until you are truly mine—otherwise—"

Tensely Iva repeated, "Otherwise—."

"Otherwise we must begin the fight at once to see which is the stronger, my Father—or myself."

Ota gave the girl he loved no time to make a comment. "You, Iva, must decide. Will you stay here secluded until the time comes for me to take you to the Temple? Erda can instruct you in all that is necessary and in this Round Room you will be safe.

"There are two other alternatives. We can trust to my protective thought-band and you can have the freedom of the Palace; and lastly I can announce your presence to the Great Mind and tell him

I have given you my belt. It will mean war, but war between us is inevitable. Now, my love, choose you."

Iva hesitated, "I do not want to bring you trouble and war."

"That will come eventually. It must, when the Great Mind learns he has been robbed. He may already know, in which case there will be no question of deciding. But if you can choose, what will you?" Ota's face plainly showed the gravity of the occasion.

The time had come, and Iva, with all the backing of her ancestry, spoke firmly, "For my part I would not like staying in this room—alone. I want to be with you and see all the wonders of your Palace. I think I would choose the first alternative and rely on your thought-band. But it is really you, Ota, who should decide. What is your wish?"

Ota did not hesitate. "War at once," he announced his decision. "I see no use in waiting."

A slow smile curved Iva's lips. Her dimple came into view but she veiled her eyes from him as she said, "Except, Lord Ota, that in my world a maid likes to be wooed. Even though I may already be won, I would like to be courted. If you go forth to war, all the time before the six Red Suns' pass will be gone and I should have no wooing."

"We will have forever! Truly, all my life I will woo you, Iva."

"Once I am wholly yours, it will be different. Besides, suppose you were not here on the forty-second day? Everything is so strange and new to me. Oh, Ota, I beg of you to wait!" Iva threw herself on the floor at Ota's feet.

He leapt up and raised her in his arms. "So be it. For forty-six days Ota will woo his Lady. Then when I may truly call you 'Wife', together we will fight the Great Mind."

Chapter VIII
In the Banquet Hall

The next three days—or talas, as Ota called them—passed quickly for Iva. From the time when, after their talk in the Round Room, Ota had hurried her back through the secret passages to his own chamber and then ostentatiously had Erda conduct her back to the room she had been given for her own, Iva had been busy. She practiced the language with Erda, for although the blue girl could not speak, she could understand perfectly and shook her head if Iva made a mistake.

Everything was done for her comfort. The women who had been with her when she first awoke, were all her slaves, and the entire women's quarters were turned over to her under the superintendence of Efa.

Efa was a strange creature. Age in this Land of Youth was considered, apparently, a repulsive thing. The other women shuddered at her approach. Even Erda turned her eyes away. To Iva the wrinkled and ancient appearance of Efa only served as a reminder of her own grandmother, despite the fact that at seventy she had been far younger-looking than Efa. Still the faint resemblance made Iva take the older-looking woman to her heart, and Efa, who at first had regarded Iva with disdain, thawed under the warmth of the Earth Girl's advances.

From Efa Iva learned many of the customs of the Blue Land. She learned that there were no fish nor birds upon Venus, but there were many animals which she must see to know. Some were very fierce and dangerous; others, like the horses, were devoted to their masters.

The Gardens of the Palace of the Four Towers were entirely free from animals of any kind and kept so by the guards, so that it was always safe to walk or play in the acres that surrounded the Palace. There were beasts resembling cows on a gigantic scale, whose milk furnished a drink for the household which tasted something like a combination of absinthe and honey but had no intoxicating effects and yet was very strengthening and stimulating.

It seemed particularly strange to Iva that these people never slept. Efa explained that while the Red Sun was in the heavens they had no need to repose, but that during the one tala there was no sun, everybody slumbered. Iva, used to sleeping part of each twenty-four hours, still continued to do so, but found each day that she needed less sleep. Efa said that soon she would adjust herself to the Venusian ways and sleep only on the seventh day, and Iva was sure it would be so.

Already she had become accustomed to one meal a day, which is how these strange people were served. At what would ordinarily be midday, the entire household assembled in the huge Hall. At one end was a raised dais, at which Iva sat with Ota and a few of the other men and their wives. Below were tables for the rest of the Court, at which the members were seated in accordance to their rank. The first day Iva had appeared among them, they had all risen and shouted out her name in welcome. Later Ota told her that that very morning he had assembled his Court together and that he had announced to them that he had given his belt to Iva, the Earth girl, whom the Great Mind had brought to their planet.

At first there had been murmurs of horror at the disobedience to the Great Mind, but then he had told them that he planned to overthrow the absolute Ruler of Venus, and with one mighty voice they had hailed him and Iva, professing their loyalty. The very fact that Iva had been amongst them so long and worn the belt without a blow falling, gave them confidence in Ota and made them willing to agree to anything he might ask. A full report of this gathering was also given Iva by Efa.

The meal consisted mostly of the milk from the cows—Iva called it milk although anything more unlike milk she could hardly imagine—and a queer kind of breadish cake, with plenty of fruit.

The fruits resembled nothing that Iva had ever seen upon Earth, but were perfectly delicious. When she asked Efa if they never ate animals, Efa was horror-stricken. "Would one eat a friend?" she cried. "Are not our animals friends? Do they not supply us with drink and transportation? Even the wild animals we would not harm."

Iva said nothing, but in her heart she admitted the justice of the outburst. She had always thought killing anything that lived, inhuman, but she would never have suspected to find her ideas crystallized on Venus.

She saw very little of Ota. They met at the daily meal and he visited her once a day, and once during the twenty-four hours Erda ostensibly escorted her to pay a ceremonial call on Ota. But after they passed the guard who stood before Ota's quarters, they traversed the tiny passage and made their way to the Round Room. Here Iva experienced heavenly moments in Ota's arms, but they were necessarily short, for to no one did Ota wish the secret of the Round Room revealed. Besides, as he carefully explained to Iva, he needed every second of his time to prepare for the battle that would come.

With this arrangement Iva was content. She, too, realized the importance of Ota's being ready to fight his Father, even while she regretted the necessity. Besides, she was interested in seeing the entire Palace under Efa's guidance, and knew that the forty-two days that must pass would not be enough to see it all. She did this too partly because she noticed that whenever she went off with Erda, there was a difference in Efa's manner when she returned and that it took her some time to coax Efa back into good humor.

At the meal on the fifth day of her arrival in Venus, Iva turned to Ota. "My Lord," she said, "neither of us seems to have had the idea of appealing to your Father. Surely if he knew of our love—."

Ota's laugh cut short her words. It echoed through the Banquet Hall and was taken up by the others in the room for the sheer infectiousness of its mirth. Before the final echo had died away, however, Ota's face changed and became more serious than Iva had ever seen it.

"Oh, my Love, you little know the Great Mind! Have I not told you that here on Venus there is no family feeling? My Father would no more hesitate to crush me than he would to press a flower, nor would the fact that we love mean anything to him. He could more easily throw me into the fiery furnace and watch me burn, with pleasure, than he could forgive my disobedience in even the slightest way. And this that I have done is crime unspeakable."

"I'm beginning to understand," said Iva thoughtfully. "Tell me, Ota," she continued, "if I displeased you, what would you do to me?"

"You could do no wrong nor could I punish you if you did. Such is my love for you," he replied promptly.

Although she had asked the question lightly, nevertheless, she felt a sense of relief over his response. In a land where there was no family feeling and fathers cared nothing for their offspring, perhaps even Ota's love might—her thoughts were broken into by her lover's voice.

"For the first time I have read a thought of yours," he was saying. "Your Earth mind, being tuned differently to mine, has hitherto made it impossible, but just now you were wondering about my love, contrasting it with my Father's lack of feeling. Is it not so?"

Abashed, Iva hung her head in consent.

"Fear not. Did I not tell you we love the women we take to our heart and the friends we choose for ourselves, and those who win our affections?" Ota asked.

"But perhaps you love other women," stammered Iva, voicing at last a matter that had troubled her ever since Efa had exhibited a part of the Palace that would correspond to the Harem of an Eastern Potentate. Efa had said it was for the slaves and concubines and assured Iva it was empty, but Iva had wondered. She had felt too, that rather than share her man, she would welcome death.

Ota swallowed a glass of the absinthe-like liquid before he replied, "For Ota there has never been and never will be any woman but Iva. There has been no other woman who counted or whom I cared for, in all my life. Did I not swear it so by the Red Sun?"

"You swore to take none for your wife, but you said nothing of slaves—or—or—concubines."

"I said 'all women on our planet', and so it has been. Before that I played with passion, never love, my Iva." Ota's words were like caresses and Iva's heart beat faster.

Just then from afar came the note of a bugle. Noa, who with his wife Gertrada was dining with them, sprang up, but at a look from Ota resumed his place.

"You do not will that I should go?" he asked.

Ota shook his head. "It may well be only one of the nobles I have sent for. We will wait."

Several days before, he had told Iva that he had flashed the signal from his towers that summoned all his subjects to the Palace. They would have to be there at the ceremony in the Temple and it was well to have them near, under his more immediate protection.

Iva had found life in the Palace of the Four Towers very much as life must have been in Versailles, to which it had such an outward resemblance. Ota had a regular court and his nobles all had quarters allotted to them for their wives and slaves. The Palace was a miniature world in itself.

At the first note of the bugle, Erda, who always sat at Iva's feet, drew closer, and Efa who had been eating at a table far away, slipped up behind Iva's chair. If Ota noticed, he gave no sign.

A sudden silence swept over the huge Hall. A breathlessness and hushed expectancy fell upon the hitherto laughing throng.

Iva wondered what would happen next and even as she did so, two guards came in at the Great Door and walking the length of the Hall, halted at the foot of the dias facing Ota. They raised their right arms high above their heads and said simultaneously so that it sounded as though there were only one voice, "A Messenger awaits without, Lord Ota."

Ota answered their salutation by inclining his head. "From whom comes this Messenger?" he asked calmly.

And through a silence so intense that Iva could hear the gasping breath of the woman Efa behind her, came the answer, "The Messenger, My Lord, is from the Great Mind."

Chapter IX
Another Alternative

Without an instant's hesitation, Ota's voice rang out, "Admit the Messenger from the Great Mind."

Even now there was no sound in all the Hall save the tramp of the guards' feet, but Iva could feel the wave of fear that swept over everyone and sensed their tense attitude. She oould read nothing from Ota's expression. He seemed to be concentrating intensely and Iva supposed he was working some spell or strengthening an old one.

The woman, Efa, crept up between the chairs occupied by the Ruler of the Blue Land and his Lady. "Master," she whispered, "shall I not take your Lady to her chamber? Perhaps if she is not seen—"

Ota waved the woman away. "If I had meant to do so, I had long since sent her with Erda. Hold your peace."

As the woman fell back with an angry flush, he turned to Iva. "It is too late to hide you now—the Great Mind Knows!"

His words made Iva catch her breath and drove the sentences she had been about to speak from her mind. She made no sign to show her fear, although she was deathly afraid. Perhaps Ota sensed this for he laid his hand over hers where it rested on the arm of the throne chair, which was exactly like the one he occupied.

Then suddenly came the tramp of sandaled feet and through the door came six of Ota's guards. In their middle walked the strangest looking man Iva had ever seen.

He was tall, taller even than Ota, and his hair was a brilliant emerald green. His skin was yellow, his eyes deep blue, the ends of his fingers were crimson and through the thongs of his sandals Iva could see that his toes from the joint on were also red. He wore the now familiar loin cloth and a belt studded with all four stones. His features were sharp and there was an unpleasant look about his full red lips.

When they reached the foot of the dais, the guards stepped aside and the Messenger advanced a few paces nearer to the steps. Iva and Ota faced him with the long, narrow table between.

He made no salutation. He merely stood silently waiting for some word from Ota, and Iva felt his keen eyes surveying her.

Finally Ota broke the tension, "Greetings, Oh Messenger from the Great Mind, my Father, ruler of us all."

"Yet whose rule is perhaps not acknowledged by the Lord Ota," returned the messenger evenly, without taking his eyes from Iva.

"Has the Ruler of the Blue Land so spoken?" asked Ota.

The Messenger for the first time looked at Ota. "The Great Mind knows, and so does the Lord of the Blue Land, that speech is not always necessary."

Ota moved impatiently, "You have a message?" he questioned.

The Messenger's eyes returned to Iva. "I have, My Lord, and it concerns this creature whom you have set beside you."

Even the Messenger shrank at the tone of Ota's voice. "Beware how you speak of my Lady and my wife, or I shall burn you where you stand. Speak your message gently or not at all!"

Erda put her hand on Iva's knee and Iva leaned forward to pat the girl's soft hair. As she did so, she noticed a fierce gleam in Efa's eyes.

Just then the Messenger began to speak and she forgot to make the same gesture towards the old woman. Of late she had noticed that the woman was very jealous of the girl, and had been careful to be strictly impartial.

The Messenger spoke slowly, "This is the word of the Great Mind: 'Say to my Son, Ota, Ruler of the Blue Land, that he has greatly sinned against me. He has not only taken unto himself the slave I called from another world, but he has made her his First Lady. Also, he has shut his thoughts against me and has told me nothing of these things. Only by my magic did I see him give her the belt, for I have had no communication from him. Ask him to tell you the reason for this and ask him further if there is any reason why he should not lose his belt?'"

A low murmur of horror swept through the Hall. But in Ota's face was no sign of fear.

"And if Ota does not answer these questions?" he asked.

"I am to tell you from the Great Mind that if you have an excuse worthy of his ears, he might forgive you when you deliver his slave to him." The Messenger put untold meaning into his speech.

Ota's hand grasped Iva's more firmly. So hard did he clasp it that the pressure hurt her fingers. Yet she did not flinch.

Presently he replied briefly, "Say on."

The Messenger continued, "If you bring this Earth Girl whom he has summoned to our planet, unharmed to him before the next red sun has set, he will hear your excuses and give you fair trial. The girl will go into the women's house. My master wished me to tell you," And here the messenger turned to Iva, "to have no fear for he saw you soon after your arrival and found you pleasing."

Iva bit her lip and answered nothing. If she had not been so deeply concerned in all this, she would have enjoyed the spectacle immensely—the great Mediaeval Hall with the huge tables filled with half naked men and women, was barbarically beautiful. Already Iva was at home here. To ever leave this haven would be hard, and the thought of the Great Mind filled her with unutterable loathing.

The man at her side stirred restlessly, "And if I do not comply with these demands?"

His words trailed off into space leaving a blank which the Messenger promptly filled.

"Then at the dawning of the second red sun from now will the Great Mind advance with his armies and the armies of the Green, Red and Yellow Lands, to annihilate you and your followers. Not a belt shall be left in your kingdom. The Great Mind will, of course, then take the Earth Girl to himself."

Terror swept over the entire room. Iva could read it on the faces of the people below. Only Ota and the messenger remained unmoved.

There was no hesitation on Ota's part. "Return to my Father," he cried, "and tell him I love this maid whom he summoned from another world, and she loves me, that I have given her my belt and thirty-seven days from now I take her to the Temple to seal the vows, and then she will be mine—mine, and no other man's."

A low murmur went through the Hall. Iva sensed that it was a mingling of admiration and at the same time disapprobation of his boldness.

Ota went on, "And say, too, that I fear him not. Not even if he brings all the forces of Venus against me! My men will fight with me, but not even single-handed would I fear to fight for the woman I love."

A wild yell broke out from the people in the Banquet Hall. With one accord they rose from their places, raised their right arms and cried, "Ota!" three times, until the room rang with the reverberations of their voices. Then as an afterthought they called out, "Iva," several times; and having thus expressed themselves, they resumed their seats.

"I thank you for your loyalty," said Ota and a smile was on his lips. "Nor need you fear that your confidence is misplaced." Then he turned to the Messenger and cried fiercely, "Get you gone back to your master and deliver my words!"

Discomforted, the Messenger looked at Iva. "Truly, a pretty face can stir mischief and bring trouble upon men," he announced stentoriously, then unexpectedly knelt at Ota's feet. "Your message shall be delivered, Lord Ota, but I crave permission to wait here for the tala when the red sun is set. Then with the dawn of the new sun I shall be off. Have I your leave to stay?"

Now Efa again plucked at Ota's sleeve, but he shook her off. "Aught else were discourteous. My guards will take you to the Gate House where you may rest until you leave."

The Messenger rose. All his arrogance seemed to have returned, "Perhaps before I go, you will have another message to send," he suggested, and then added, "Think well before you defy the Great Mind. Personally I advise you to send the girl with me to plead your cause. Perhaps you might be forgiven if she were pleasing enough."

Livid, Ota faced him. "Go!" he cried, and there was that in his voice that made the messenger shrink back. "My message is unaltered but go you before I forget that a messenger is safe according to our laws!"

The guards closed in about the bearer of the Great Mind's word and without further speech he permitted them to escort him from the room.

No one spoke until they had entirely disappeared from view. Then a little excited babel of conversation broke out all over the Hall and Ota, with the first sign of humor Iva had seen him display, said to her, with a merry twinkle in his eyes, "You see, there was another alternative, after all."

Chapter X
Iva Trusts Too Much

Much later in the day Ota sent the token to Erda which meant he wished Iva brought to the Round Room.

Erda found Iva reclining on the large couch that formed the principal furnishing of every room in the Palace of the Four Towers, listening to Efa.

"It is true, Lady," the old woman was saying, "nothing can hurt us but fire; therefore our soldiers carry sticks that are made of something that burns the flesh."

"Can you not be cut?" asked Iva.

The woman shook her head, "It heals immediately. I could cut off my hand and it would immediately rejoin itself. I would not even feel it. The only danger of the knife is that if my hand were taken away and buried, I would be crippled until I found the place where it was hidden. Some of the obscure tribes still fight so and hold parts of their enemy's body for ransom."

"I should think you would bleed to death," Iva remarked pensively. Then she saw Erda and the Blue Girl exhibited the token to her behind Efa's back.

"I do not know what you mean by that," the old woman was saying. "Blood is a word unknown to us."

Iva cut her short. "I will explain someday. Now I must go. Lord Ota has sent for me."

The old woman rose and seeing Erda, pushed her aside. "I will take you, Lady," she cried."

"Erda will escort me," Iva answered firmly. "You must await me here."

"No, no!" screamed Efa. "It is my place to be with you! Am I not your instructress? Are you not kind to me? Am I not the one you love?"

Now Iva was in a predicament. She did not dare let Efa come with her, for the secret of the Round Room was known only to Erda and Iva knew very well that the last thing in the world Ota would want would be for the old woman to suspect its existence.

Several times she had suspected that Efa was jealous and that the devotion the old woman lavished upon her was far too intense. She had meant to speak to Ota about this, for she had twice seen Efa look at Erda in a way that boded no good to the Blue Girl. Now she heartily wished she had done so, for Ota would have known how to deal with the present situation. As it was, she must handle it as best she could.

She gently patted Efa's wrinkled cheek. "My Lord has sent Erda for me, so I must go with her. Another time, perhaps, I can take you."

"I will never leave you. I must be at your side unless you are with Lord Ota, Lady. Come, we will go. She," and with scorn in her voice the woman indicated the Blue Girl, "can follow."

Erda shook her head frantically and made a clicking sound with her fingers that summoned the other women. Surmising Erda's intention and fearing the old woman's wrath for the girl, if Erda had her held captive, Iva quickly seized Erda's hand. "Come," she cried, and then to Efa, "Follow if you will."

Erda tried to make frantic signals but Iva pressed her hand reassuringly.

The trio made their way in silence through the halls until they reached the guards before the small door which led to Ota's chamber. Iva pushed Erda through. Then before Efa could follow, she said to the guards, "Let no one pass until I return. Efa, await me here." Then she quickly followed Erda through the door.

They waited until the door was shut and they could no longer hear Efa's protestations, before they made their way down the secret passages. Iva made a silent resolve to tell Ota of the old woman's actions the minute she saw him, but when the door opened and Ota swept her into his arms, she forgot everything but the joy of his kisses.

"Ia dorva sea," he whispered over and over, and Iva cried it back to him. The soft, musical, "ia dorva sea" with the lingering accents on the "a" which was pronounced more like "ar" was, to Iva, even more beautiful than her own language, "I love you," although the meaning was the same.

For several moments they clung together, the Blue Man bending over Iva, who fortunately was a good height herself. Before she had been transported to Venus, Iva often had wished she could subtract a few inches from her five feet plus, but now she wished she could add several inches, for her head only came to a little below Ota's shoulder.

With a sudden gesture, Ota lifted her in his arms and carried her to the couch. He sat down upon it and held Iva as though she were a baby.

"Are you afraid, little Earth Child?" he asked.

Iva shook her head and murmured, "Ora," the Venusian equivalent of "No."

"You need not be. I sent for you for two reasons; first because my eyes were hungry for a sight of your loveliness, and second because in a few hours the red sun will set and your first Venus night will be upon you. Sleep well, my love. Have Efa wrap you in a long mantle and have no fear for while you sleep I shall be working out a new spell which I have just found."

Ota smoothed Iva's soft hair with his free hand. "If I am able to wholly decipher it, then I shall have the Great Mind in the hollow of my hand. Truly, those ancient ones who have passed, were great masters of magic."

"How does it happen that they—passed—when on Venus there is no death?" questioned Iva.

"There was a stage in our planet's development when everything was consumed by the fire of the red sun. So went these ancients. Their books survived because before the heat became too intense, they buried the books in a metal box under the river. It was there Ula found them quite by accident as he stooped to drink, oh, most curious one!"

For a minute they laughed together, then Ota relapsed into seriousness. "All the night I shall be working, and perchance the next tala. Then I will send for you, either here or to my chamber. I only wanted you to know what I was doing, for I shall give out word that I work in my chamber and must not be disturbed. And of course during the night I shall not be missed."

"Cannot I stay with you?" pleaded Iva.

"No, my love. Do you think I could work as hard as I must with such distraction near?" He leaned over and kissed her mouth.

After all she knew Ota to be right. Later they would stand together, and in the meantime she would be patient and try to still the gnawing fear in her breast, fear of the Great Mind and that in some way he would separate her from Ota, Ota whom she loved so much.

The thread of her thoughts was broken by the object of them. "Now you must go," he was saying. "Go and prepare for night, and take my love and my heart with you, for they are ever yours."

He carried her to the door. Before he set her on her feet, he kissed the soft red lips again, and to Iva it felt as though he drew her very soul into his being. Then quite suddenly he released her and, opening the door, called Erda.

The blue girl sprang up and he placed Iva's hand in hers. Then he said, "Guard well my Lady," and with his right arm raised in salutation, stepped back into the Round Room, and the door swung shut.

Long after Iva remembered his words and wondered if they had been prophetic. At the time a sense of utter desolation swept over her and she shivered a little for no reason. In Venus the climate was perpetually that of a lovely June day, and by now her skin had become accustomed to being exposed.

When Efa greeted her, she recalled that she had not spoken to the Lord of the Blue Land about the woman, but then Efa was so pleasant that she promptly dismissed the matter from her mind. The old woman said nothing about the way she had behaved, and Iva was only too glad to let the matter rest. She noticed that it was growing dark almost like an earthly twilight.

"Have you no lights?" she asked.

"When the Red Sun sets, the whole of Venus sleeps," Efa told her. "Even the Great Mind rests his brain cells; we therefore need no light. The guards have little torches that shine in the dark if necessary, but they are rarely used."

"Radium of some sort," Iva thought. Out loud she told Efa to bring her a mantle.

The old woman obeyed and brought a gorgeous wrap of some strange material that was like velvet, in which she enveloped the earth girl. Then she heaped pillows on the couch and said, "If my Lady will recline, I will cover her and then bring a soothing drink. Hurry, for there is little time left now before the light goes."

Iva, who was tired, gladly followed the old woman's suggestion. Erda had already curled up on some cushions at the foot of the couch and was apparently sound asleep. The other women were sleeping in the next room, for Iva had several chambers for her own use.

Through the transparent side of the room, which Iva faced, she could see that the sky had become a deep, purplish red, so dark as to be almost black. Iva could just distinguish a faint blue ray from one of the Towers. She was watching it when Efa returned with a goblet in her hand.

Iva stirred wearily. "What is it?"

"Just the drink that you like, my Lady, so your throat will not be parched in the long night." Efa held the goblet nearer.

Iva took it and swallowed half of it, then gave the glass back to Efa. It was the same wine-like liquid that she was served in the Banquet Hall but it tasted less sweet than usual.

The old woman leaned over her. Through the darkness Iva could just make out her form. "Sleep well, my Lady," she heard her say, and there was something in her tone that Iva had never heard before.

"Where will you be, Efa?" she whispered, and as in a dream she heard the woman's voice, "Fear not, my Lady, I shall be near." It seemed to come from far away, and still had that strange note in it, almost a triumphant sound. Iva wished she could see the woman's expression, but now utter blackness had descended.

"Efa!" she called, but heard no response. Iva gave a little sigh of perplexity, then her eyes shut and she lapsed into a deep, dreamless sleep.

Chapter XI
One More Strange Awakening

Iva opened her eyes. Instead of the soft blue walls and ceiling to which she had grown accustomed, there was an inky blackness. She supposed it was still night and as she felt uncomfortable, she decided to turn over.

To her amazement, she found she could not move, that she was securely bound; and at the same time she realized that she was not lying on her soft cushions but on a hard, flat surface.

A wave of terror swept over her. Where could she be? Had the Great Mind triumphed already? Was she in his power? She tried to scream, but there was a gag in her mouth—she could make no sound.

"God," she prayed, "save me." And then she began to wonder. Was her God powerful on Venus or was he solely the God of Earth? Surely he must be universal. Thoughts rushed in and out of her brain like the waters of many streams. Where could she be? What had happened? Did Ota know?

She turned her head a little. Far off she could see a tiny pin point of light. As it came nearer, it grew larger, until presently she saw that it was some kind of torch. She could not see who carried it, for behind its blaze all was dark. Its rays illuminated quite a space in front, and she perceived she was lying in a sort of cave.

Presently the light flashed full in her face. She shut her eyes against its glare while a wave of terror swept over her. What would be behind this blaze of light? The Great Mind with the aid of light had brought her to Venus, so surely this must emanate from the Great Mind too. Little tremors shook her which she could not control.

Through her closed eyelids she felt the direct force of the light taken away but there was still illumination. She heard a slight noise and judged the torch had been set down at some point of vantage. She had no courage to look. She wanted to postpone the evil moment as long as she could.

She felt hands fumbling around her mouth and to her great joy the gag was removed. She gasped with the relief of feeling the cool air in her throat, opened her eyes and looked up—

Bending down over her was Efa.

"Were you taken, too?" she cried.

The old woman laughed and Iva noticed a strange gleam in her eyes. "My Lady," she whispered, "My Lady, no one else's! From now on you belong to me, and to me alone!"

"I don't understand," murmured Iva weakly. "Who brought me here?"

"I did." The woman struck her flat bosom. "I carried you through the dark palace. I held you while the multan brought us to this cave. I have put the multan far inside where his neighing cannot be heard. So we are safe."

"But why? Why did you do this?" Iva's mind was groping for understanding.

"You are mine, I tell you! The others, Ota and Erda, tried to keep you from me so I took you myself, and I will keep you from them. Never will they find us and we will be happy together, you and I!" Efa took Iva, all bound as she was, into her arms and rocked her back and forth as though she were a little child.

Iva began to understand. She had been kind to Efa and her kindness had aroused an almost fanatical devotion in the old woman's heart. Efa had been jealous of Erda. When she had been prevented from following them that day, the jealousy had boiled up and poisoned her—and this was her revenge.

Iva looked into the old woman's eyes and read madness in them. Very bitterly did she regret not telling Ota of the woman's behavior. Now he would be at a loss, with no clue as to her whereabouts. He would probably think Efa had been abducted too, and blame the Great Mind, just as she had done.

A sudden thought struck her.

"Efa," she began carefully, not to rouse the insanity she was sure governed the woman, "You have done wrong taking me from Lord Ota. You will deliver us both into the power of the Great Mind."

The old woman shook her head.

Iva persisted, "Only Lord Ota can save us from him."

"Think you I am a fool? Did not your lover bind my thoughts? Besides, the Great Mind would never think of me, and your mind he cannot contact. We are quite safe and you are mine, my Earth Child, and no one, not even the Great Mind himself, shall take you from me!"

The girl shuddered and the old woman, thinking she was cold, drew her closer and swayed back and forth in a monotonous fashion.

Iva did not give up. "We will starve here," she suggested.

Again the old woman shook her head. "I have provided for that. Here," she patted the bag that hung from her belt, "Here I have food pellets. We will only need one for each red sun. Then in the night we will ride until we reach my own country. No one will ever think of that, for on the whole of Venus there is no one else who would dare to travel by night."

"My Lord Ota will find me," cried Iva proudly. "You had better take me back to him, for if you do not, when he finds me you will lose your belt."

"I would not care; besides," a crafty light shone in the woman's eyes, "When we reach my country, I shall take your belt from you as mine was taken. You will grow old like me, and then Ota will not want you—no, nor the Great Mind either! I would do it now, but you will need strength for the journey."

Horror for the moment kept Iva silent. On earth she had never dreaded old age, never even given it a thought, merely accepting it as an inevitable happening that came to all. But here, here on Venus, the land of Eternal Youth, to be old, to see Ota shrink from her, would be more than she could bear.

Desperation gave her an idea. "I am of Earth. I could do perfectly without my belt—it wouldn't affect me!"

"We shall see!" cackled the old woman. "We shall see."

Iva tried to move. "I am very uncomfortable. Must you keep me tied up like this?"

With quick hands the old woman undid the fastenings wound around Iva's slim body. "It was only while I was carrying you from the Palace that these were necessary. Though I had given you a sleeping draught, I feared that you might wake and rouse the guards. I left you tied while I took the multan back farther into the cave. Here, take this food pellet." She set Iva free and reached into her bag, giving the girl a round white tablet.

At first Iva was going to refuse, but then, seeing Efa eating one, she took hers and chewed it. There was no taste, but almost immediately Iva's hunger was satisfied and she felt stronger. She knew she must keep up her strength, for she intended to escape at the first opportunity. To do so she must find out her present local-ity, without arousing Efa's suspicions. So walking up and down to limber her stiff limbs she asked, "Where is your country?"

"Twelve suns from here. It will take us three nights to reach it. It lies at the farthest corner of Ota's land. The multan carried us well. We went at least a thousand versts," the woman said proudly.

Iva knew that a verst was equal to about two earth miles. So they were five hundred miles away from the Palace of the Four Towers. She could never cover that distance without the multan. She must watch Efa carefully and discover where she had hidden the beast. Then in some way she would have to mount it and win her freedom and her love.

"Ota!" her heart cried, "Ota, come to me!" Almost it was more than she could bear. She sank on her knees before Efa.

"Oh, Efa," she cried, and the hot tears fell down her cheeks, "take me back. If you love me, take me back to my Lord. I cannot live without him. I will protect you and love you, only take me back!"

The old woman stared at her in amazement and fell back a few paces. "Is this a magic that you do? Would you flood this cave with water from your eyes?"

Iva seized at the idea. "Truly, that I will do unless you take me back!"

For a few seconds Efa hesitated; then she laughed and the weird cackle of her laughter sent shivers of horror through the Earth Girl's body.

"If you do not stop," she yelled, "I will burn your eyes with the hot stick and then you will never see your love again."

The tears stopped falling. "And you say you love me!" the girl cried scornfully.

"I do, I do. But you are mine, and rather than lose you I would torture you—yes, or kill you."

After this announcement the woman sank on her knees and began mumbling to herself so fast that Iva could make nothing of what she said, but supposed it to be either some magic or invocation to the Red Sun which these people all worshipped.

Iva herself walked round and round the cave. It was circular with several dark and narrow passages leading from it. The torch, which resembled an electric flashlight, gave out a tremendous light. The old woman had set it on a ledge from where it threw forth a blue light that illuminated the cave but left the passageways dark. Without it Iva knew she could never find her way; so she mentally added it to the multan as something to be taken.

She walked over close to the torch and observed it more fully. It was round at the end, almost the shape of an apple and covered with the same transparent stuff that was used instead of glass for windows on Venus. It was apparently not electric, for the handle part was too narrow to hold a battery. Iva thought perhaps it might contain radium, and later found that her guess had been correct. She was to discover also that the Venusians had developed the use of radium to the highest degree.

Iva put her hand out towards the torch. Her action made the old woman stop her mumbling. "Do not touch that!" she cried.

"Why?"

"It is at just the correct angle, and you might disturb it."

"Will it not go out?" queried Iva in the soft biblical language to which she had now grown accustomed.

"Never! In fact, it grows stronger as the aeons pass." The old woman seemed calmer and her eyes looked normal for the first time since Iva's awakening. "Come," she beckoned, "come and lie with your head in my lap so I may comb your hair."

Iva came and did as the old woman suggested. She had decided to humor her; then later perhaps he could get the woman to sleep, for surely she must be weary, as she had no sleep during the night.

Soothingly the comb passed through Iva's curls. "It is so soft, your hair," crooned the old woman, "softer than the finest of silks, and the color is unlike anything I have ever seen. Truly your world produces surpassing beauty. Are all the people like you?"

"I'm just average." For the moment Iva lapsed back into the vernacular. Then she went on and told Efa about the Earth. She talked a long time in a monotonous voice, and as she went on she noticed that the old woman's eyes were heavy.

While Iva was in the midst of describing the beauty of Joan Crawford, the first person who came into her mind, the old woman stopped combing and leaned back against the wall, letting her head rest upon it. Iva pretended not to notice but went on talking softly. She told stories of Joan Crawford which would have surprised even Joan's press agent, by their ingenuity. Long after the old woman's eyes had shut and her breathing became slow and regular, Iva continued. Once she stopped a second and the old woman moved. After that she continued, but her words no longer made sense.

Still talking, she moved ever so slightly.

The old woman slept on.

Iva very gently lifted her head from the woman's lap and still talking moved her hand until it came in contact with the rope which had been tossed carelessly aside when Efa released her from her bonds.

For a moment she debated whether she should tie up the old woman or just steal away, but finally decided that only the first was practical, for there was the multan to be found. Very softly and gently, while she sang the charms of Joan's Hollywood House, she put one end of the rope behind Efa's back. There was quite a hollow in the wall, which made it easy for Iva. Then with great care she brought the rope across the old woman and made a slip-knot on the side. Then, with a silent prayer, she stopped talking.

The old woman stirred, and Iva, with every ounce of strength she possessed, pulled the rope tight. It now completely encircled Efa and bound her arms to her sides.

With a sudden start the old woman awoke and struggled to her feet. Iva, quickly running around her while she fought, soon had her encased in the rope, somewhat as a mummy is swathed, except there were gaps between, where the rope wound around.

The old woman screamed with rage. "Untie me!" she yelled over and over.

"Never," returned Iva. "Where is the multan?"

"If you free me, I will show you."

Iva saw the cunning gleam in the blue eyes and shook her head. "I will find him without your help and he will take me back to my Lord, but first I will make you more comfortable." She knotted the loose end of the rope around Efa's foot, then laid Efa gently down alongside the wall of the cave.

The old woman was light, and it was easy to do, but in a frenzy of rage Efa tried to bite the girl.

Iva sprang back. "I will leave you," she cried, "but I will leave you food pellets where you can reach them by turning your head. I would not have you starve." She reached in Efa's bag and from several other kinds of tablets selected the food ones, which fortunately were easily distinguishable from the others by their size.

She laid them within easy reach of Efa's shrivelled lips. Three she kept for herself, tying them in the corner of her silken skirt which was drawn through her belt.

"If you will tell me where the multan is, I will come back for you," she whispered, "and I will protect you from my Lord's anger."

"I pray the Red Sun sends you to the Great Mind," the old woman hissed.

Iva gave up. "Then I must leave you in the dark while I find the multan," she said, ignoring the old woman's curse.

She walked over to the torch. She grasped its tiny handle and then with its light in front of her, went towards the direction from which she remembered the light originally had come.

She had hardly gone more than thirty steps when she heard Efa cry, "The Red Sun be praised!" Then the old woman's laughter shrill and high, pierced echoing in her ears.

She turned, fearing the old woman had perhaps worked her way free. The light which she held downwards in her hand, showed her a man's foot in a blue sandal. She turned the light upwards and then gasped with horror, while the light fell upon the floor from her trembling hand.

For leering down at her, in that one swift moment of illumination, she had seen the face of the Great Mind's Messenger.

Chapter XII
Ota Makes a Mistake

Throughout the long night Ota sat poring over one of the huge
books of the Ancients. Hour after hour he turned the pages,
rapidly memorizing their contents.

Often the sweet face of the earth girl came between his eyes
and the crabbed hieroglyphics and for a few seconds Ota would
think of the girl he loved. Then quickly he would banish her image
from his mind and return to the spells he was learning in order to
protect her.

At length the letters became so blurred he could no longer distinguish one from the other. He had trained himself to need very
little sleep, but now his eyes were becoming heavy and nature's
demands were no longer to be ignored.

He woke up suddenly, roused by a frantic knocking at the door.
The sound was faint, for the door was thick, but its impatience was
unmistakable.

Ota sprang to his feet. His first conscious thought was that
perhaps the Great Mind—

Quickly he swung back the door and Erda almost tumbled at
his feet. She regained her balance and in her excitement clasped the
Lord of the Blue Land's arm and began pulling at it.

Ota rightly interpreted her gesture to mean she wanted him to
come with her. Together they left the Round Room. Ota stopped
to pull the door shut behind him.

"Did my Lady, Iva, sleep well?" he asked.

The girl, Erda, sank down and beat her head upon the floor.

Now Ota was seriously alarmed. He had never thought of danger to Iva in his Palace, which he had considered perfectly safe. He raised Erda and stood facing her.

"Think what you would tell me," he said, and the Blue Girl nodded.

In perfect silence Ota read her thoughts. At first all he got were her lamentations that she had no tongue to speak with but then he learned of Iva's disappearance, that when Erda had awakened she had discovered the girl's couch was empty. She and the other women had searched frantically for any trace of their Lady and found none. Then she had come running for him, as no one else could have found him.

"Where did you sleep?" Ota asked.

Swiftly the girl's thoughts answered, "At the foot of my Lady's couch. Yet I heard nothing."

"And Efa? Where was she?"

Now the girl's mind was less clear. "She was not there when I went to sleep and, Lord Ota, she is not there now. I thought, perhaps, you had sent her on an errand."

Ota shook his head and taking Erda's hand he led her swiftly through the long corridors. When they reached his chamber, to which no one had the right of admittance but Erda, he quickly threw his sleeping-pillows about on his couch to make it look as though he had slept there, then he told the Blue Girl to admit the guards.

His commands were speedily obeyed. When the guards were before him, he issued crisp orders and presently the men were off to search every nook and corner of the Palace.

While they were gone, Ota looked in his divining bowl but he could see nothing at all. This he did not understand. Always he had been able to see every inch of his domain in its waters, but now only a cloudy surface met his gaze. He knew some counter magic was at work and was more sure than ever that the Great Mind was responsible for Iva's disappearance.

He sat silent, endeavoring to throw his thoughts to Iva wherever she might be, but with no success. This, however, did not surprise him. Only once in the Round Room that day had he been able to penetrate her thoughts. Her earth mind had not yet responded to his, though her heart was entirely his own. This was merely a question of adjustment to the mental vibrations of Venus, which would take time. At least, it protected her from the Great Mind's thought invasions.

After a while, the guards returned one by one, some with no information to impart, others with entirely superfluous things to tell. One and all they brought back the report that they found no trace either of Iva or of Efa.

Finally a guard from the outside came, bringing the head of the stables with him. They raised their right hands in salutation as they stood before Ota. He signaled to them to speak.

The guardian of the Stables took the lead. "Lord Ota," he said slowly, "The finest multan of your herd is gone."

Ota tossed back his red locks, "Is there aught else?"

"One thing more. The multan of the Messenger from the Great Mind is also gone."

The guard broke in, "The Messenger has departed too. No one heard him go but, of course, the men slept."

"Henceforth, in all my land, let there be two guards awake throughout the night, for short intervals. It can be done in relays. That way there will always be a guard in the night, since quite evidently the old custom of everyone staying in their places while the Red Sun is gone, has been broken. See to it." Ota hardly heard the guards murmur, "To hear is to obey," he was so engrossed in his thoughts.

At last he roused himself and asked, "Did none see the Messenger go?"

The guardian of the Stables answered, "No, My Lord, his multan was gone when I awoke."

"It seems strange that no one heard the multans; that the Messenger could go quietly and unobserved I understand, but the multans and my Lady—" Ota's voice broke.

From among the ranks of guards before Ota, a man came forward. It was Noa, who commanded the Palace Guards. He dispensed with ceremony.

"Lord," he cried, "I believe the whole Palace was drugged. I know I have never slept so sound, and my Lady, when the Red Sun dawned, said she felt very strange. Perhaps a drug was placed in the drink. We all drank to toast you and your Lady after the Messenger had left the Hall."

Ota slapped his hand upon his knee. "My friend, you have spoken. Nothing else could account for it. In some way the Messenger must have drugged the drink. I see it all now. This is a plot of the Great Mind's to take my Bride from me. While the whole Palace slept—a deep sleep from which there was no danger of their awakening—the Messenger undoubtedly stole into my Lady's sleeping room and carried her off."

Noa nodded his head, then quite suddenly asked, "But Efa, why did he take Efa?"

"Perhaps the old one did not fall under the influence of the drug. Perhaps she drank nothing. She must have tried to prevent his leaving with my Lady, and to silence her he undoubtedly took her along, knowing she would tell all and that thus we would be the quicker on his trail." Ota was very calm, but anguish was easily visible in his eyes.

"The other multan was undoubtedly taken for Efa to ride. He probably bound her to the multan's back and carried the Lady Iva himself," was Noa's contribution to the solving of the mystery.

Neither of them had the faintest suspicion of the truth. Not once even, did it cross Ota's mind that Efa might have abducted the girl he had chosen for his mate. He knew nothing of the old woman's jealousy, and Erda, who had never thought of it as being important, did not mention it. Neither did the two guards who had heard the old woman scream when Iva had shut the door so she could not follow. These, the only people possessing the sole clue, said nothing, ignorant that their knowledge would have given the key to the situation.

As his friend mentioned the Messenger carrying Iva, Ota shut his eyes, remembering how he had carried her in his arms on the multan's back the day they had first met. Even now the thrill of the feel of her slender body in his arms swept over him, but the thought of other arms encircling her brought fury in its wake.

Ota leapt to his feet. "Now, by all the Ancient Gods and the Red Sun," he cried—and his great voice shook with emotion—"it shall go hard with that messenger. He shall know the torture of a thousand burnings. And I swear, by the sweet curls of my Lady's hair that the Great Mind, himself, shall know the fury of my wrath and suffer from it."

Even the stalwart guards paled a little before their Lord's oath, but Noa quickly rose to the occasion. He leapt to the couch from which Ota had risen and standing upon it raised his right hand. He said feelingly, "So be it! We cry allegiance to our Lord, and vengeance to his enemies!"

The right arms of everyone in the room rose, and as one man they echoed Noa's speech.

Ota put one hand upon the shoulder of Noa. His right arm answered the salute.

"So be it," he said. Then more slowly, "The Lord of the Blue Land is grateful. Go now and make ready, for in less than one ga (the Venus equivalent of an Earth hour) we march to Gecca and face the Great Mind in his home. Get all in order and bid farewell to such of your women who are not fit to go. The others march with us. We will leave a small guard here for emergencies.

Quickly the guards dispersed. Noa would have followed, but Ota's hand still gripped his shoulder.

Ota now turned to Erda. "Go you too," he told her gently. "You and your women stay here to make ready for your Lady's return."

Erda sank on her knees before him and raised her hands pleadingly, utter misery in every line of her at his ultimatum. Her love for Iva made her forget that to question her Lord's command or plead against it, was a grievous offence.

In one second Ota read her thoughts. "I see," he said kindly, "you want to go with me to your Lady. So be it. I cannot deny you for your very love of her whom I love beyond mention. Make ready quickly to depart. The rest of your women stay."

Erda waited for no more. She swiftly kissed Ota's hand and was gone.

Ota and Noa were left alone. After a short silence, Ota said, "My friend, I have kept you with me because you, of all others, I trust and love. Ever since I became ruler of the Blue Land we have been comrades and have grown close, bound by the ties that only friendship makes."

"It is true, my Lord. I love you as I love no other man."

"So it is with me. To you, Noa, if I am caught in the web the Great Mind spins, I give my Lordship of the Blue Land. Of a truth it is yours by right, since my Father took it from yours." Ota's lips curved ever so slightly, but the anguish in his eyes belied the smile.

Noa shrugged his great shoulders, scarcely less broad than Ota's own. "I want nothing more from life than I already have. When my father reigned, I was miserable, but in your company I have gained happiness. I ask no more. Your bidding I will ever do. Both my Lady and I are yours to command."

In the silence of the Blue Lord's sleeping-room the two men shook hands, not as earth people do but by clasping each other's wrists. And in that clasp more was said than all the words that had heretofore passed between them.

Then Noa asked, "What now?"

Slowly Ota answered him, "Two things. On the way to the Tower I shall tell you my plans for the war that must ensue to win back my Lady, and when we have reached the highest Tower, for the first time since Iva came to Venus I will speak the Oracle and open my thoughts to the great Mind!"

When they were half-way up the winding stairs of the Great Tower, Ota turned to his friend.

"Wait for me here. Venture not another flight unless I call. If I have not returned to you in half a ga, then you may ascend."

Noa bowed and left the stairway. At intervals there were rooms all the way up the Tower, and to one of these Noa went. Usually guards were stationed in front of the transparent part of the wall, which in the Towers were smaller than in the sleeping-rooms. But today they were empty as the men prepared for the march and the battle that was to come.

Noa's thoughts were busy with that battle, for Ota had revealed some of the plans he had made; not all, for not even to Noa did the Blue Lord dare to tell the coup that he relied upon to conquer the Great Mind. But despite this he had told Noa enough to give him plenty of food for thought.

Suddenly Noa heard steps on the stairway. Before he had time to leave the room, Ota stood in the doorway. He looked gaunt and worn and physically exhausted.

Noa ran to him and putting his hand under Blue Lord's elbow asked, "What news?"

Ota's seemed sunken far into his head. His breath came in little, short gasps. Between them he stammered, "I sent my thoughts far but I established contact with no one. I could not understand, not even the thought wave from Efa's mind could I find. Then I spoke the all-powerful word that opens the channel of thought communication between my Father and myself—and nothing happened—nothing!"

Noa waited. Presently Ota spoke again. "The Great Mind knows too, how to render his thoughts invulnerable. Without doubt he has Iva in his power. We must march quickly, gathering our people as we go, for if the messenger reaches Gecca with Iva before we do, there will be no hope. Only I can protect her from the Great Mind.

"Pray, pray, Noa, to the Red Sun that the Messenger meets obstacles upon his way. Otherwise, there will be nothing left for us to hope for but—revenge!"

Chapter XIII
The Messenger

For one terror-stricken second after she had seen the face of the Messenger, Iva stood still. Then she swung around and began to run down the dark corridor. "Better the unknown than surrender," she thought.

But that one second betrayed her. She had hardly run six feet before the quick strides of the Messenger overtook her and she felt his great hand close over her wrist.

Now her screams echoed through the vaulted cavern and mingled curiously with Efa's laughter. Iva tried to stop screaming but could not. All the bravery she had had since her arrival on Venus seemed suddenly to have deserted her.

The Messenger pulled her back into the cave none too gently. Just once he stopped to retrieve the torch. After he had it in his free hand, their progress was speedier.

Presently they were back in the cave. By now Iva had gained control of herself. Biting her lips she had forced back the screams and attained, at least, the semblance of calmness; only on the surface, however, for her heart beat furiously and her thoughts flew about from one thing to another like leaves scattered helter-skelter by the wind.

The great, ungainly form of the Messenger towered above her and dwarfed the cave, herself and Efa into diminutive proportions by comparison.

Efa stopped her laughing as they approached and looked up at the Messenger.

"Truly, the red sun sent you to my aid," she cried.

The Messenger said nothing, but his lip curled back over his teeth. He reached into a bag hanging from his belt and drew out a thin, silken cord, made of twisted strands of the four colors that Venus knew. Curiously it reminded Iva of a necklace she had bought a year ago in Paris.

Paris! What a far cry it was from Paris to Venus—Paris, the most luxurious city of modern civilization, and Venus where everything was so entirely different. To Iva it seemed strange that she did not long more for her own world. Even now, in this terrible situation that she was facing, if she were given the opportunity to return to Earth, she would refuse on the chance of Ota's rescuing her. She dimly wondered why this was so, but accepted it because she knew it was the truth. Ota was her world and like Ruth, his people were her people forevermore.

Iva was entirely a one-man woman. Moreover, she was the type of those who, when once they love, surrender utterly to their affection. Fortunately for her this was so, for Ota had taken the place of home, parents and friends, and taken it adequately. She had been perfectly content but now—

Her thoughts were broken by a sudden movement of the Messenger. He had made a noose of the twisted cord and deftly slipped it over Iva's head. Before she had quite grasped what he was doing, he had pulled it tight around her throat. She raised her hand to take it off, but the Messenger's voice stopped her.

"Is it uncomfortable?"

"No," Iva admitted. As a matter of fact, it was so light she could not feel the cord at all. "But I don't like the idea," she went on.

The Messenger brought the loose end down and twisted it around her belt deftly. It hung freely between Iva's breasts.

"I wouldn't try to take it off, if I were you," he said. "Then it might become very uncomfortable. The more you try to loosen it the tighter it would grow."

Iva's hand dropped. "But why?" she questioned.

"Because, as long as I hold this," he held up a small, square metal object, "you can't get away. Try to move farther than ten feet."

Iva began to walk. Her progress was free and unimpeded, but when she had reached a distance of what she judged was the aforementioned ten feet, she felt the cord tighten about her neck, and like a living thing it gave a shrill whistle.

"Come back," called the Messenger, "a few more feet and it would strangle you, and until loosened it you could not breathe, which would be uncomfortable, at least. It's a little scheme of my Master's whereby he insures the proximity of anyone he is not quite certain of. He can regulate the distance he wants them to go away from him."

"I see." Iva's head drooped. She could see no possibility of escape unless by some lucky chance she could procure the stone (or whatever it was) which in some magic way acted as a magnet to the thing about her neck. Just now it looked pretty hopeless for the Messenger was putting the magnet back in his bag.

Still, Iva did not despair. Alone and unaided she had gotten the better of a half-crazed woman. Perhaps whatever was guiding her destiny—God, Fate, or circumstance—would permit her to escape from this danger also.

Efa spoke again, "So, my Lady betrayed Efa! Well, much good it did you." She laughed loudly.

"You dare not talk to me of betrayal," cried Iva, "You who betrayed not only me, but my Lord, Ota. He should have known you better from of old and never trusted you who were so little worthy!"

"Fine talk. Fine talk. But you will not talk or carry your head too high when you face the Great Mind. Then you will wish you had stayed with me. And I shall laugh at your sufferings, laugh—like this!" And peal after peal of her wild, maniacal laughter filled the cavern.

Iva cowered back. The old woman had spoken one truth. She had much rather stay with her, even at the risk of growing old and wrinkled, than submit to the Great Mind's caresses. Better death than that. But in this strange land she could not die. She must live on and suffer. For the first time Iva questioned the joy of an everlasting life. Truly she would be in hell unless Ota found her or she, herself, discovered a way to win free from this dilemma.

The voice of the Messenger interrupted her thoughts. "Cease your laughter," he bellowed forth.

There was silence in the cavern as the old woman obeyed him.

"Where is the multan?" the messenger asked sternly.

"I cry a bargain." Efa's voice was soft and there was a cunning gleam in her eyes. "My freedom for the multan."

The Messenger laughed. "Have I not feet to walk with, eyes to see with, and a torch to light my way? I need no bargains, woman."

"The Earth Girl might escape while you searched. She is sly and cunning. Look how she got away from me, though of a truth she never would have had I not drunk a little of the drink into which I put the sleeping potion, for fear someone might suspect me, and thus my eyes grew heavy." The old woman went on, "My freedom for the multan!"

Again the messenger laughed. "You are old and foolish. The Earth Girl would follow me. She must for her own sake or else lie strangled and breathless until I come near to her again. I have no fear for her."

"Nor need he have," thought Iva. Truly she was caught, like a butterfly in a net, and helplessly she would beat her wings upon it unless by chance she could discover a way to slip through. Well, she would not despair, she would wait until she found a weak spot in the net. If she could not, when they neared the Great Mind, she would try to take off her belt and grow old, as Efa had threatened. At least, the Great Mind wouldn't want her if she were a wrinkled hag like Efa.

A sudden thought hurled itself upon her. Neither would Ota! Well, then she would die. But she would not attempt such a desperate solution of her problem until all hope had failed, for she was sure that somehow or some way Ota would find her.

"You had better tell me," the Messenger was saying. "I make no bargains, but I might reward you if you save time for my Master, who grows impatient for the Earth Girl. Truly, I do not blame him. She is well made."

His steely eyes swept over Iva, and she swiftly turned away from him.

But Efa began to speak and her interest in what was happening made her forget her lack of attire.

"Go along the center corridor," Efa was saying. "Take the second turn to the right, the next left turn, and you will find another cave, where I have left the beast. Could you not free me and loosen the cord from my Lady's throat and leave her here? This time I will guard her well."

"Think you I have no wits? Come, Lady; you, old woman, await us as you are." The Messenger signaled to Iva to follow him. The girl had no choice but to obey.

Efa croaked out, "But my reward! You promised me a reward."

For a second the Messenger paused. "You will have a reward when my Master learns all. He has cause to be grateful to you. Without you the Earth Girl would not have fallen into his hands until he had captured her in battle. Now he will wage war all the better. Truly, you will be highly rewarded."

"Good, good!" cried the old woman. "Unloosen me now that I may foretaste my triumph."

"That I cannot do. Here you must stay until I send for you. I cannot delay for one instant my going to Gecca with the Earth Girl. Two on one multan makes slower progress. No, woman, you must wait here—and I must waste no more time." The Messenger strode forth down the corridor with Iva following.

Efa's screams grew fainter the farther they walked. Iva felt no sympathy for the woman as she recalled her threats, but she felt that she would rather have Efa than be utterly alone with the Messenger.

Timidly she spoke, "The woman is very light. I do not think her added weight would impede the multan's speed."

"The matter is settled. We go without her. When I speak to the Great Mind, I will ask his instructions. But I dare not do otherwise, now," answered the Messenger.

Iva's heart sank "Are we near to Gecca?"

"No. Why do you ask?"

"You said you would speak to the Great Mind." The Earth Girl's voice trembled.

Without slackening his speed, the Messenger replied, "Every tala, on the stroke of the fourth hour, the Great Mind communicates with me. Our thoughts meet. Then I shall make a full report to him and he will be overjoyed to know I bring you to him. I will then tell him of the old woman, but I cannot wait two gas; therefore we leave at once."

"How do you know what ga it is?" asked Iva. She felt she must gather all the information possible, for there was no telling how much knowledge she might need for the escape she would endeavor to make.

"Do you not know?" he asked in his turn.

Iva shook her head. "I have no watch to tell me the time."

"Watch? What is that?"

Iva explained, then asked again how he knew what time it was.

"All of us on Venus know instantly whenever we wish. In Gecca there is a great machine, perhaps like that of which you tell me, only it is huge in size, which sends out the ga throughout the Kingdom. We have only to think and we receive the emanations. Now—" he paused a second, then went on, "It is nearly the beginning of the second ga."

"How simple," thought Iva. "Truly, these inhabitants of Venus have developed many things to the nth degree. They knew much that was just beginning to be dimly suspected on Earth—the power of their minds."

Not allowing her thoughts to be side-tracked, she went on with her questioning. "Can you not call the Great Mind before the fourth ga if you need him?"

"In a great emergency I could, but this is not one," the man told her.

To her "How would you do that?" he made no response, and before she could press the matter, they had arrived at the inner cave where the multan was standing quietly.

With a start of surprise, Iva recognized the great beast as the one Ota had ridden the day she arrived on Venus. It had a star-shaped mark between its eyes which she had not forgotten. A hot tear fell down her cheek as Iva remembered that ride in Ota's arms.

"Mount," said the Messenger briefly.

The horse knelt without a word being spoken. Iva gently patted the place where the star was, and it seemed as though she could read sympathy in the multan's eyes. Then she climbed upon his back, for even kneeling, its height was great.

Sitting sideways, Iva held on to a strand of the multan's blue mane. The Messenger led the way back to the outer cavern. When they reached it, he stared about in utter astonishment, for no sign of the old woman was to be found in the cave.

One of the food pellets was visible near where she had lain, but of Efa, herself, there was no trace.

Chapter XIV
On the Way to Gecca

Both Iva and the Messenger looked at the spot where the old woman had been, in utter amazement.

The Messenger broke the silence. "You tied the knot fast?"

"Certainly. She must have tried to undo it while I went for the multan—and it held then, I mean before you came." Iva started to slide off the multan's back but the Messenger prevented her.

"We must hasten with all speed possible to Gecca. In all probability she has taken my multan which I left outside, in which case we will needs go slowly."

"Are you not going to search for Efa?"

"No. I can waste no more time. Most like, she will go to the Blue Lord." The Messenger signaled the multan to follow him and walked quickly to the entrance of the cave. It was quite a distance, and on their way Iva prayed that the old woman had had a change of heart and gone to Ota. But her mind rejected the joyful possibility as she remembered the hatred in Efa's eyes. Iva was quite sure on reflection that Efa would rather see her delivered to the Great Mind than safely returned to the man she loved.

The Messenger's multan neighed joyously at their approach. The Messenger spoke a few quick words to him, then turned to Iva, with a puzzled expression on his face.

"I do not understand," he said, "but doubtless my Master will explain all." He vaulted to his multan's back—no mean feat in itself, when the multan stands at least twelve feet high.

A few seconds more and they were rushing over the blue grass at the speed which Iva could never get used to from the back of a horse.

Of course, the multans of Venus were superhorses in every way. But to be on a horse's back, traveling faster than the average motor would go on Earth, was almost unbelievable to Iva, even while she was doing so.

All at once a thought struck Iva. They were riding in daylight. Efa had planned to travel only at night. Surely now that the red sun was high in the heavens, Ota would see her in his divining bowl. Of course, it would take him a long time to make up the distance Efa had carried her throughout the long Venusian night, but she had faith in his powers and knew that somehow he would find the way.

A kind of contentment settled over Iva, she was so sure of her Lord's powers. Of course, she had no knowledge of the fact that the Great Mind had rendered Ota's divining bowl quite useless.

Iva, in her ignorance, constantly looked back for the first sign of her Lord. Finally she addressed the Messenger.

"Are the multans your only means of transportation?"

"What more do we need?" was his answer.

Iva could have told him of some of the other methods used on Earth, but she did not. Instead, she looked about the surrounding country. It was so beautiful, the rosy sky, the red sun and the blending of blues! Iva remembered a friend who had worked for years to achieve a blue garden, and the small field of flowers of that color she had to choose from. While here were thousands of varied blooms, each a different shade. The whole effect was like some lovely stage setting, unbelievingly beautiful. Joseph Urban or Maxfield Parrish might have conceived the country through which she was passing, but no one else could have, except its Maker.

Suddenly it dawned upon Iva that they had passed no villages. "Are there no towns on Venus?" she asked.

"Towns? What are they?"

"Cities?"

Still the Messenger looked blank.

Iva explained. "I mean clusters of houses, dwelling-places grouped together in which various families live, which on Earth we call a town, city or a village."

"Here we call such a thing a cluta. There are many. The largest is Gecca where the Great Mind lives; the next is Ota's cluta which is called Ulla, after its former ruler who founded it. There are many more clutas on Venus, but we are not passing through them. The Great Mind wishes us to reach him quickly, so I take the shortest way through the open country." The Messenger lapsed back into silence.

Just then, in the distance, Iva saw a group of long, low buildings. "Look!" she called excitedly, "That must be a cluta!"

The messenger shook his head. "Not at all. That is one of the breeding-houses."

"Breeding? What do they breed? Multans?"

"Men and women," the Messenger told her laconically.

"What?" Iva almost stopped the swift pace of the multan in her astonishment.

"What a strange place your planet must be," the Messenger mused. "I will explain to you and then you must tell me how your earth people produce your progeny. Here twice a year our women bring forth a spawn, or duna, sometimes of six or eight potential children—never less than two or three—although on rare occasions there have been instances of only one duna. These are always brought to life as they, being more concentrated, are better citizens. Your Lord Ota was such a child."

"Brought to life?" interrupted Iva. "Are they not alive when they are born?"

"Certainly not. They have only potential life. They are very tiny, about the length of my middle finger. They are at once taken from their mothers to the brooderie. Here the majority are placed in storage. If the parents at that particular time desire a child, one or two are put into the life-giving brook where they slowly grow and eventually come to their natural size. When they have grown to be about three feet, they are taken out of the brook and kept in dormitories where they are given the pills of knowledge and understanding and learn fellowship. When they have grown to be five feet and are of an age to be intelligent, they are given out to homes."

"But are they not given to their own mothers even then?" Iva questioned.

Patiently the Messenger went on, "In the case of important people, they are sometimes, if it is so requested. But it rarely is.

Of course, in the case of the rulers or high Lords, their offshoots are raised separately and always returned to them. But otherwise it matters very little, since up to the time they are given to the people, they are all alike. The storehouses are full, but these duna are kept for emergencies.

"In the event of a war or a terrible fire, then the dunas are allowed to grow to take the places of the people who are wiped out. Naturally, the size of families must be limited or with our unending term of existence, Venus would be overrun with people.

"Three is the largest number of children any one family can have at one time. It is the law. Every hundred gatras our people can have a new family if they like."

Iva knew a 'gatra' corresponded to an earthly year.

"It is necessary that all married people raise at least one child during that time."

"I should think even your storehouses would be overcrowded," said Iva, doing simple arithmetic in her mind.

"When a duna reaches the age of five hundred gatras, it is destroyed. So we keep the storehouses always about the same capacity and the dunas fresh."

"What a people!" thought Iva. No wonder Ota had said that she would understand why there was no family feeling on Venus, when he had time to explain. She understood now and wondered that men and women reared in such a way could be capable of affection at all.

The voice of the Messenger broke into her thoughts, "How do you manage to raise children on Earth?" he was asking.

A low laugh broke from Iva's lips, the first time she had smiled since her awakening. The idea of explaining the process of child-bearing to this huge man was too much for her sense of humor.

"It is much too complicated to make you understand," she told him. "But on Earth we women bear one child at a time—sometimes only one in our whole lifetime—and we love it with all our hearts."

"How strange!" remarked the Messenger, "and what a waste of love! Love should be only for the one we mate with—and the friends we choose."

Evidently this was the Venusian philosophy, thought Iva, and in its way a good one, especially under the existing circumstances.

She lapsed into silence, but she looked at the low-lying buildings with their surrounding water which was worked into lagoons and partly walled off, with great interest.

They passed by quickly. At the high rate of speed the multans traveled, it was impossible to get more than a vague idea of the buildings which must have covered at least ten earth miles.

"You must be able to swim if you spend the first years of your life in water," she broke the silence. Somehow, the whole system reminded her of fish hatcheries, and the Venus system of life seemed to her to be patterned after that of fishes on Earth.

"Of course," answered the Messenger. "We love water. We spend several talas in it often."

"You mean you can breathe under water?" gasped Iva.

"Naturally."

"Amphibians!" thought Iva, and then wondered if that were the name she meant. Her simile of the fishes was certainly more correct than she had imagined. She wondered if she, too, would be able to breathe under water, to spend a day beneath the sparkling surfaces. She hoped so, for she loved to swim. She could hardly wait to try. She was sure now that her body was adjusted to Venus and that she would be able to. She would get Ota to go with her. Ota! She caught her breath in a little sobbing gasp. Ota! Where was he? Why did he not come? Perhaps she would never see the man she loved again.

Chapter XV
The Fourth Ga

For a long time they rode on in silence. Iva hung tightly to the multan's mane and sat well towards the horse's neck. Even so there were moments that she was afraid she would lose her balance. She had always been considered a wonderful horsewoman, but then on Earth she had had harness and stirrups to aid her. Here she had nothing but the thick mane to cling to, and the speed at which they traveled was terrific. Her only consolation was that the multan's back was quite as broad as any ordinary roadster on earth would have been.

Iva looked over at the Messenger sitting up straight, perfectly balanced, and marvelled. She thought of the Centaurs and compared him to those mythical beings.

Suddenly the Messenger made a little clicking sound and the multans began to slacken their pace. It took them a little while to check their speed, but after a bit they were going at what seemed to Iva a normal trot. Now the country looked more beautiful than ever and she could observe many details.

They were nearing the edge of a wood, row upon row of slender, straight-limbed trees that suddenly spread out into a wealth of foliage. The effect was almost like an umbrella. The leaves were of a rich, cobalt blue and the lighter blue sward and underbrush with the deep purplish trunks of the trees, made a picture of breath-taking loveliness.

Iva was on the point of exclaiming when the Messenger gave another guttural sound and the multans came to an abrupt stop.

The Messenger swung one leg over and slid to the ground. "It is near the Fourth Ga," he said simply, "when I will communicate with my Master. You may get down and rest if you wish."

He stretched out his great arms and assisted the girl to reach the ground. Then he led her a little way towards the trees. In the shadow of one of them he suggested that she might like to recline.

Iva welcomed the suggestion. Only now did she realize how physically exhausted she was. So she stretched herself out upon the blue grass and relaxed for the first time since her awakening in the cave.

The Messenger looked at her coldly. "Do not think because I am abstracted, that I am not watching you; nor that the cord will lose its power—never as long as I possess this stone." He put his hand upon the bag which hung from his belt.

Iva made no reply. She realized only too well the hopelessness of her situation. Somehow or some way she must procure the stone, but how she could not quite see. At the moment there was nothing to do but rest her aching body and hope that sometime she would find an opportunity.

She lay back comfortably and watched. The multans stood quietly, almost as though they were statues. The Messenger walked about six feet from Iva and then sat cross-legged on the grass. He made no preparations but seemingly relaxed into a kind of trance. His eyes, however, were wide open and focused upon Iva. So remembering his words, she made no effort to move.

The Messenger's expression did not change, nor did he move.

"I might as well be with a group of Madame Taussaud's figures," thought Iva.

Then all at once an idea came to her. Perhaps in this land where thoughts were so important, she could make her thoughts be of help to her. Somewhere Ota must be trying to make his mind contact with hers. Perhaps if she concentrated, she might get in touch with him. Once he had read her thoughts and surely two people who loved each other as intensely as she and Ota loved, ought to be en rapport.

Iva shut her eyes and sent her thoughts forth. "Ota, Ota!" she repeated over and over. "Ota," she called soundlessly into space. But there was no response.

The Great Mind's magic was powerful when not even love could break its way through his spells.

Iva was so lost in her endeavor to send her thoughts to Ota that she did not notice when the Messenger rose. Only when the shadow of his huge body fell over her did she again become attuned to her present surroundings.

"We must be on our way," he said curtly.

Iva rose a little wearily. She had ridden farther than any earth muscles could have done. The fact that she could do it and feel only the slightest fatigue showed Iva that she must have become one of the Venusians. She idly wondered if now, like them, she was utterly dependent on the belt that Ota had given her, and supposed it must be so.

The multan came at the Messenger's call and knelt near Iva. Except for the hump, the process reminded Iva of a camel she had once ridden in the London Zoo. As a matter of fact, the multans rather resembled camels as far as size went, except that they were broader.

Iva settled herself well near the animal's neck and patted it gently before she grasped its mane in her hands. The multan neighed softly and rose carefully to its feet.

"What did your Master say?" began Iva, then stopped short and half turned to see what the Messenger was doing.

From his seat on the other multan, with his huge hands he was pushing along Iva's multan's back behind Iva, a stout stick which stretched across the multan. Presently a thud was heard which sounded like some object striking the ground. The Messenger called out a word and the multans galloped off.

From behind them came screams which became fainter and fainter as they rode on. Iva, looking back, had at no time seen anything. She looked at the Messenger inquiringly.

He answered her unspoken question. "It was the old woman. While we searched for the multan in the cave, she managed to get loose from her bonds and then from her bag she took the tablet of invisibility and swallowed it; There are only a few of these tablets on Venus and most of them are in the Great Mind's possession. Either the woman, Efa, stole this one or got it from Ula. At any rate, invisible, she rode with us on the back of your multan. So much space was between you that you were not conscious of her presence."

"Indeed, I had no idea," gasped Iva, "but the multan, did he not know?"

"Of course. But he could not tell. Our beasts understand certain words we have taught them, but they cannot speak."

Iva nodded her head and her curls fell over into her eyes. She tossed them back. She did not dare take her hands from the multan's mane and risk losing her balance.

"My Master saw all," the Messenger went on. "Moreover, he knew she but bided her time to spirit you away to her own land, and my Master, wishing no further delay to the hour when he clasps you in his arms, bade me sweep her from the multan and leave her behind. This I did, as you perceived. She may meet with Ota and tell her tale if she wills. My Master cares not, although later he will reward her for making your capture easy."

The latter part of the Messenger's speech was lost to Iva. She got no further than the words, "She may meet with Ota," Meet with Ota! Then her Lord must be on his way to her! Gladness flowed over Iva as the waves of the ocean go over a bather who stands in their path. She had known Ota would come, but the positive knowledge that she was followed, gave her a sense of security.

Somehow she must delay their progress. If she could engage the Messenger in conversation and perhaps retard the pace of the multans by pulling on the mane of hers, she might give Ota a chance to catch up with them. She gave a little tug to the thick purplish hair, each strand of which was the size of her little finger. To her joy she was rewarded by a slight retardment in the speed of her mount. She knew the other multan would accordingly slacken its pace.

Now for the second part of her plot. She turned to the Messenger. "What else did the Great Mind say?"

"Did I not tell you? He bade me hasten, for he longed to hold you in his arms. His other instructions were for me alone; the way we should travel. You will find out in time. Of a truth, for the first time I envy my Master!" His eyes swept over the girl's slender form, leaving no doubt as to his meaning.

Iva bit her lip. At all costs she must keep her temper and occupy the thoughts of this man. Already by pulling at the multan's mane, she had checked the high rate of speed. But her only hope in continuing to do so was to keep the Messenger busy talking. She must find some topic of conversation.

Her glance searched the road ahead for something of interest about which she could ask questions, but around her were only the slim trees. For now they were in the woods, on the edge of which she had rested. The trees were very thick and so close that their branches interwoven formed a leafy roof, entirely shutting out the glow of the Red Sun. There was a blue light, however, which came from the trunks of the trees—between these trunks was very little space.

They were following a road which had been cut through the forest. Far away she saw a thread of smoke. She pointed to it, "Is that a cluta?"

"There is no cluta in these woods," the Messenger said curtly.

"But," persisted Iva, "surely that is smoke and where there is smoke there must be a fire."

Now the Messenger looked in the direction she had indicated. Iva, watching him, saw the color drain from his face and terror follow in its wake, terror such as Iva had never seen. In one second this big, strong man became like a helpless frightened child.

"What is it?" cried Iva, still looking at him.

With chattering teeth he answered her. "It is the Fiery Beast. Not even the Great Mind can save us now."

Chapter XVI
Another Road

Scarcely three gas, or earth hours, after the discovery of Iva's disappearance, Ota and his followers were on their way. Ota rode first on the swiftest multan of his stables, with Noa on one side and Erda on the other, mounted on steeds almost as fast.

Behind them came Ota's men with their ladies by their sides. Straight and firm the Venus women sat upon their horses, as staunch as any warrior or Amazon could have been. The concubines or women of amusement were left behind, but these, the chosen of their husbands, rode with them to share their fate.

Before they passed through the gates of the Palace of the Four Towers, Ota turned his multan so that he faced them all.

"I want each of you to wear an apron that shall now be given you, and each to carry in your belt a strange new weapon. I do not tell you its use now, for when we pass these gates your thoughts will be as an open book to one who can read them. You are to put the weapon through your belt as it is given you and on no account touch it until I tell you what to do."

A great sound wave came to him. "Hearing is obeying," they said as with one voice.

A rare smile broke over Ota's face. "My people," he said gently, "We go against one who is all-powerful, but have no fear. We will meet the Great Mind and we will not be defeated!"

There was a great cheer and Ota heard his name shouted over and over. He gave the signal to the men of his body guard, who opened large boxes that a short time ago they had carried from his sleeping-room. Ota, himself, had brought them there from secret cupboards in the Round Room. For years he had been laboring to discover what the boxes contained, with the conviction firmly in his heart that some day they would be needed. Well, the day was here. Never would they be needed more. He had found out their use just in time.

Ota leapt from his horse and followed by Noa, went to a smaller box. This he opened and took out an apron made of some strange-looking material, in one piece, with a large round opening. It slipped easily over his head and was held by a narrow band round his neck, and two straps which fastened at the waist. It covered the entire front of his body from his neck to a little above his knees. His hips, too, were partly covered, but his arms were bare and there was nothing in the back except the narrow bands about his neck and waist.

He then took out a long tube-like object covered completely by the same material as the apron. It was about two feet long, with the circumference of an orange. This Ota slipped through his belt under the apron. The belt, being like elastic, stretched enough to hold it comfortably but firmly.

Now Ota called to his people among whom the aprons and tube-like objects were being distributed.

"Do thou likewise." And with his own hands he placed an apron upon Noa and fitted the weapon into his belt so all could see.

While they were obeying his instructions, he took out still another set from the box, and yet another, which he handed to Noa. "For your Lady, Gertrada and for Erda," he said shortly, and stood staring into the box where one more apron and tube remained.

"And that?" questioned Noa, pointing to the almost empty box.

"That was for Iva," Ota answered with a break in his beautiful voice. Then he took a square of silk and folded the apron and tube into a bundle, almost like that a gypsy uses to carry her belongings. This he took and fastened securely to his multan's mane with one of the horse's thick hairs. "At any rate," he half whispered, "it shall be ready for her. And by the Red Sun, I pray that she may wear it!"

Then he spoke loudly to one of his men, "if any are unused, we will carry them so for those who join us." He indicated the bundle tied to his multan's mane and the man departed to give the orders, while Ota sprang upon his multan's back.

Noa followed his Master's example. "My Lord," he asked, "what way do we ride?"

Ota hesitated before he spoke, but finally responded, "The straight road to Gecca."

Noa's Lady, Gertrada, whose multan was close by, leaned towards Ota. "My Lord, have I your leave to speak?"

Ota nodded.

"Then I crave your pardon for questioning you, but do you know what road the Messenger chose?" Gertrada was very beautiful—next to Iva, perhaps the loveliest woman on Venus—and ordinarily it was a joy to Ota to look at her, but at the moment s he might have been as ugly as Efa so far as Ota was concerned.

He turned and gazed at her with pain in his eyes. "I would give all of my possessions if I but knew."

Gertrada went on, "Then do you not think they would go a less frequented way, one they would think you might not suspect?"

Now Ota made his second mistake. He judged his Father by his own impatience. Of course, he knew nothing of Efa's hand in Iva's capture. He expressed his thought to Gertrada.

"The Great Mind would surely instruct his man to go the quickest way. Already we have lost time. They had almost twenty-four gas' start before we discovered their absence. And I can see nothing, nor find out where they are by my magic. The Messenger will have to pause while my Lady rests. Her earthly body will demand rest and the Great Mind will do nothing to harm her."

Ota's voice became bitter. "On this I base my hope, that by riding at a greater speed than she could, constantly, we may reach them before they pass the Golden Gates of Gecca. We take the straight road."

Gertrada bowed her head. Her woman's intuition had made her speak, but now she was silent before the Blue Lord's superior wisdom.

"Are all mounted?" Ota called.

From at least five thousand voices came the answer, "Tra!"—yes. Still facing them, Ota continued, "Tied to your multans' manes is a small bag with food tablets and a flask of strengthening drink, which will be all you need, for we ride steadily until we reach my Lady, or the Gates of Gecca."

Ota swung his horse around and raised his right arm. The huge gates swung open silently. The cavalcade, with Ota at its head, passed through.

* * *

When Efa was swept off Iva's multan by the Messenger, she stood on the blue grass and shrieked loudly. In her twisted mind she thought that by so doing the Messenger would return to quiet her, fearing perhaps that she would give away their presence by the noise she was making.

But as she watched them growing smaller and smaller as they rode away from her, until finally they melted into the horizon, she stopped her screaming and began to wonder what she had best do.

To follow them would be useless. She could never hope to attain the swiftness of the multans, and she knew that the Messenger of the Great Mind would wait for nothing, not even Iva's weariness.

To gain her own land and rouse the half-savage people who were her kin, to her aid, was equally impossible without a multan to carry her the long distance.

Efa cursed herself for not having taken the Messenger's multan when she had left the cave. At the time, secure in her own invisibility, she had thought it better to ride with them and watch for a chance to abduct Iva a second time. Curiously enough, she had never thought that she would be discovered. For once she had forgotten the Great Mind, who saw all. Her thoughts had been entirely concentrated on the girl she loved.

Now only two courses were open to her; one to wait where she was until Ota came. Then either to join in with him, or try to deceive him as to Iva's whereabouts. This way she decided against— sooner or later Ota would learn the truth about what she had done, and no mercy would he shown her.

The second course was to seek out a cluta, or small town, and purloin a multan, then go to Gecca and claim her reward from the Great Mind. The reward for which she would ask would be the Earth Girl! The Great Mind tired quickly of his fancies. Once he had wearied of Iva, he would not care what became of her and he would gladly give her to Efa, who would cherish her.

Strange Awakening

With this all arranged satisfactorily in her mind, Efa started across the country walking steadily in the direction of the nearest cluta.

Chapter XVII
The Fiery Beast

As Iva wondered what new terror had come upon her, the multans gave one scream of fear and then stopped short. Iva could feel the muscles of the one she rode twitching beneath her and her own slender body rocked to the horse's trembling.

She looked again in the direction of the smoke and gasped with astonishment, for coming towards them was a dragon, its enormous head facing them, its endless body stretching on and on behind. The smoke Iva had seen was coming from its nose. At the present moment its huge jaws were shut but Iva had no doubt they would belch forth fire when they opened. The body was constructed of sequin-like scales of a blue-black color that scintillated, reminding Iva of an evening dress her mother had once possessed.

Though still some distance away, she could see the glint of its eyes. For a moment she could not take seriously the beast lumbering towards them, which reminded her so of Fafner, the dragon in Wagner's opera. She could hardly believe that this beast was not also composed of papier mache. She had always laughed so, when at the Metropolitan the dragon had come out of the cave. It had been so palpably unreal. Surely this thing—then she felt the trembling of her multan grow worse and worse, and suddenly awoke to the seriousness of the situation.

A cold perspiration marked her realization that this was a real menace. Like the dragons of old that St. George had fought, there was one before her now only there was no St. George and no Siegfried, only the Messenger. She called to him.

"We must go back. We can travel faster than the beast!"

In a voice that was harsh and strained, the Messenger replied, "We cannot move. We have seen the Fiery Beast, so we cannot move from this spot! We are marked for its prey. Even if we were not, we could not turn, the road is too narrow."

Iva had read of birds being fascinated by serpents so she dimly grasped what the Messenger meant. She saw that he and the multans were looking straight at the approaching Fiery Beast. He was now so near that she could feel the heat emanating from him.

"Can you do nothing?" she cried despairingly.

"Nothing," the hollow voice of the Messenger told her, "But await the end. On all of Venus there are but three of these beasts. Usually they stay in their lairs, except during the night. To think that my life ends so!" The Messenger began to sob.

Now the multans, too, were whining with terror.

Iva tried to wrench her eyes away from the scaly monster. Surely she did not have to wait here to be devoured! But to her utter horror, she found that she could not move her eyes.

Was this the end? Had all her perils and the transportation to Venus been for this purpose?

Ota—Ota—her love—Ota! Immersed in her thoughts of him and the love for him that filled her heart, she quite unconsciously shut her eyes.

It was not until she felt the burning heat from the Fiery Beast more intensely, that she realized she had done so.

Then, all her senses alert, with her eyes still closed, she slipped from the multan's back.

Knowing that her glance would be turned from the monster, she opened her eyes and perceived she was on the edge of the road. She wedged her slim body between the trunks of the trees. There was just room for her to get through.

Frantically she went on into the forest until all at once she felt the cord about her neck tightening, and knew she had gone the allotted ten feet from the Messenger.

"Fool!" she thought. "He might have given me the stone. Now I am tied to this spot—until—"

A new horror struck her. Suppose the dragon ate the Messenger and swallowed the stone! She would have to follow the dragon.

In the woods she could keep away from him, but once out in the open there would be no hope for her.

She turned in the direction of the road. "Throw me the stone!" she shrieked, but the terror-stricken snorts of the multans drowned out her voice.

From where she stood she could see the road plainly. The dragon was within ten feet of the Messenger and the two multans. The Messenger had mastered his terror and was fearing the inevitable stoically. Whether he knew of her departure or not, Iva did not know, as his eyes were fixed on the dragon. She believed he thought her beside him.

Now the dragon opened his mouth and sent a jet of flame at the Messenger. One minute the huge man was there; the next he was enveloped in fire; and the next there was no trace of him at all. And then the dragon's monstrous jaws were upon the multan, for the Messenger only had been burned.

Iva shut her eyes and put her hands over her ears to keep from them the sounds of that grim meal. When she dared to look again, the road was clear. There was no sign that anything had occurred nor was any trace of the dragon visible.

Cautiously Iva made her way to the road. She gazed up and down but the Fiery Beast had gone on. He must have followed the path in the direction from which Iva had come for to turn his gigantic body in that narrow path would have been utterly impossible.

Iva got down on her hands and knees to search for the stone. Frantically she felt along the blue grass until after what seemed like ages although only a short time had elapsed, her search was rewarded. With a cry of joy she struggled to her feet with the stone in her hand. The work of a second and she had removed the cord from her neck. This she carefully wound about the stone and thrust them both under her belt.

At last she was free!—free from the Messenger and from the Great Mind! She laughed exultingly. But all at once her joy died. Yes, she was free, but she was utterly alone, with no idea of what to do next.

Chapter XVIII
At the End of the Forest

In the soft blue light of the wood Iva shivered. It was not the atmosphere that made her cold. It was fear. Everything seemed so difficult and now she was entirely at a loss. What to do next was beyond her comprehension. To go forward would be to play into the hands of the Great Mind; and she did not dare go back, for between where she now stood and where Ota might be behind her was lurking not only the Fiery Beast but Efa.

Of the two Iva felt that Efa was the more to be dreaded. She was probably quite near by now. To go back would be only to fall into the old woman's clutches once more.

Two of the tears that Ota deemed so precious, fell from Iva's eyes. She wiped them away and as she did so a new idea came to her.

She would not follow the road at either end of which lay danger. She would strike off through the trees. She alone on all Venus was slim enough to make her way through the trunks that grew so close together. Doing this she would get out of the woods eventually and make her way to the nearest cluta.

Ota had said all his people would be loyal to him, so when she came to the town she would tell them who she was and demand an escort back to her Lord. She guessed that there might be flaws in her plan, but it seemed the only possible thing for her to do.

Iva stood for a minute in the middle of the road, which stretched far beyond her on either side, facing the forest. Then she walked straight ahead and began to make her way through the tree trunks.

Presently when she looked back there was no longer any sign of the road. She was entirely surrounded by the slender trunks of the trees while overhead the leafy canopy rustled softly.

Iva became more hopeful. In the back of her mind she was sure Ota could see her present whereabouts in his divining bowl, as he had seen her arrival on Venus. She was almost certain that when she emerged from the forest, Ota would be waiting for her, and in the meantime she was safe—safe from Efa, safe even from the Great Mind. By now she had decided she would not come forth from the protection of the tree trunks until she heard Ota's voice. Such was her faith in his power to find her. Not knowing of the Great Mind's counter spell, she went on dreaming joyously of the moment when Ota would clasp her in his arms again.

She had lost all track of time since she had left the Palace, but she hoped that soon the number of talas, or days, that kept her from being taken to the Temple and proclaimed Ota's wife would he over. Beyond anything she wanted to belong to Ota, to whom she had given her heart.

Iva trudged on and on doggedly, until finally her earth body rebelled and she realized she was utterly weary. She knew that she must give her aching limbs a rest, so she sank down onto the thick blue moss that covered the ground which had made walking pleasant for her hare feet.

Before she permitted her heavy eyelids to close, she took one of the food tablets from the corner of her belt and swallowed it. Immediately the hollow feeling disappeared and she felt as though she had eaten a full meal. She was remarkably satisfied. She pillowed her head upon her arm and in a few minutes was fast asleep.

Utterly exhausted mentally as well as physically by the strange adventures she had undergone since her last awakening, Iva slept soundly, a deep sleep that nothing could penetrate.

After a while she began to dream, a strange mixed-up jumble of all she had been through. Then everything faded from her mind and in her sleep the clear eyes of Ota looked into hers. "I'm coming," she heard him say, and a deep contentment flowed over her. She lapsed into the peace which this provided and for a long time slumbered dreamlessly.

Then her sleep was invaded by dreams again. She thought that Ota was building a city for her. She could hear the noise of the work of piling stone upon stone, but she could see nothing. In her dream it seemed as though the city was being built behind her and although she was permitted to hear, she could not see. She listened intensely for the sounds which grew louder and louder, until they crashed in her ears like explosions.

"I must look," she kept saying, and finally a voice came to her—a strange voice, quite unlike Ota's soft musical one. This voice grated and sounded horrible to her listening ears. In a high-pitched whine it said, "Now you can see."

With a start Iva came from the unconscious world into the conscious one. She sat up, opened her eyes and gave a little cry of terror. She was entirely surrounded by a group of vari-colored men exactly like the Messenger. Beyond them as far as she could see lay fallen trees. Her dream had been partly true. The noise which she thought was Ota building the city, had been the noise of falling trees.

She looked about her hopelessly.

One of the men came nearer to her. "We have been sent by our Master, the Great Mind, to convey you to his Palace." He put out his hand, obviously to assist her to rise.

Iva sprang to her feet unaided. She could not bear that this strange being should touch her.

"The Great Mind congratulates you on your escape from the Fiery Beast and says he will deign to learn your earth magic," the man went on.

Iva laughed bitterly. As though she could teach the Great Mind anything! Then she asked a question that had puzzled her. "Why did not the Beast eat the Messenger?"

The man looked startled but replied promptly, "The Fiery Beasts care only for animals as food. But they send any human that comes in their path to oblivion by burning them."

Now Iva wished that she had stayed on her multan. Better death, or oblivion—as they called it—than the caresses of the Great Mind.

The man in his turn asked a question, "Shall I carry you to the edge of the forest? We left our multans there when we began to cut our way through to you, as our Master ordered."

Iva bowed her head. "I prefer to walk," she said quietly, but with the accents of utmost despair in her. voice. Then, surrounded by the men from Gecca, she made her way along the road they had cut to the end of the forest.

Chapter XIX
The Golden Gates

A deep sense of unreality swept over Iva as she rode along in the center of the Great Mind's followers. These strange vari-colored men were fantastic. The blue grass and the multans were weird looking too. All was like the nightmare of a futuristic ballet master. Only Bakst could have conceived such creatures or such a land, neither Poe nor La Verue had created anything quite so bizarre.

With the Blue People she had felt at home. She had taken them to her heart because they were like Ota, to whom she had given her love. While she was with him, nothing else had mattered. And, too, she had grown fond of Erda and Efa. That the latter affection was misplaced, she knew now, but then the old woman undoubtedly was mad which accounted for her strange actions.

Iva wondered idly where Efa was now, but quickly dismissed the woman from her mind. In fact, Iva could no longer think of anything connectedly, her thoughts continually reverting back to the horror to which she was going.

Up to now she had been brave because she had been sure Ota would find her and because in each of her captures she had seen a hope of escape. Now, surrounded as she was by (she counted swiftly) thirty men, each towering far above her by reason of their great height as they sat erect on their multans, she could see no possibility of getting away from them. Slowly, inexorably, they were drawing nearer to Gecca—nearer and nearer to the Great Mind who sat waiting like a huge spider in his web for the pretty fly he had taken so much trouble to lure into his power.

Iva was in no doubt as to what her fate would be, and she knew, too, that she would rather die, rather never to see Ota again, than have it fall upon her. But to die in this land was apparently impossible.

She had had her chance when the Fiery Beast sent forth his jet of flame, but then life had seemed sweet and full of promise. Now there was no hope. Even Iva, the hopeful, had lost hope.

Ota! But by the time he came it would doubtless be too late. Perhaps—she turned her head to see if there were any sign of Ota's coming. Far behind her stretched the Blue Land but thereon was no trace of any living thing. There was no longer even any vision of the forest, only mile after mile of flat land covered with low bushes and other vegetation.

The faint ray of hope died almost as it was born. They had gone so many miles already on their swift steeds, that Ota could never catch up, even allowing for the delays: the time in the cave, the few minutes that the Messenger had communed with his Master, and while she had slept in the Forest. How long that all amounted to, Iva did not know, but she was afraid it was not nearly long enough for Ota to catch up with her before she reached Gecca.

There was no further chance of rescue, she decided, and at the same time resolved that she must find a way to die, as soon as possible. But how, in this land of perpetual life, she was to accomplish what she would regard as suicide, was quite beyond her comprehension.

Perhaps if she took off her belt? At the moment that was impossible, for she could see that the men who rode beside her were keeping their eyes focused upon her.

For the time being nothing could be done but bide her time and seize the first opportunity that might present itself. It might yet be that some new peril would come upon her and if it did this time she would not fail to take advantage of it.

"If I could only go to sleep," she thought. "Every time I wake up from a real sleep, something strange has happened. If only I could see Ota once again!" She shut her eyes in order to bring his handsome face more clearly to her vision. Now she could see the well-formed features that were so dear to her, despite their bluish tinge; the blue eyes that showed love for her in their depths, the firmly chiseled lips that had rested so softly and yet so firmly upon her own! She could almost hear him say, "I am coming," as she had in her dream.

"Ota!" her heart called, over and over, with such intensity that it seemed to her the man she loved must hear.

When Iva opened her eyes again, she gave a little cry of astonishment, for the land over which she travelled was no longer blue. Nowhere could be seen even a faint tinge of the color. The entire surrounding country—the grass, trees and flowers—was green.

For one instant Iva believed herself back on earth and that all her Venusian adventures had been a dream. But one glance at the red sky convinced her she was still on Venus. Then she looked more closely. The greens were of different shades from any she had seen on earth and everything was green, even the tree-trunks and all the flowers. Only she and her escort made contrasting colors.

She remembered Ota had told her Venus was divided into four colored lands. This then must be Pra's Green Land. It made her feel farther away from Ota than ever.

"Why," she asked the man who rode beside her, "have we left the Blue Land?"

"Because the Great Mind wishes you to enter Gecca by Pra's gateway, not by the gateway of the traitor," the man replied. Nor did he add what would have gladdened Iva's heart, that the Great Mind, knowing Ota was traveling fast and knowing also that the men of Ota 's gateway would be loyal to their Blue Lord, had chosen the easiest way to get the girl into his City of Gecca.

For a long time they rode on in silence, then all at once the man nearest Iva raised his arm. "See!" he cried, "Yonder are the Gates!"

Iva looked and saw in the distance a towering wall, in the center of which were the Golden Gates that led to Gecca.

* * *

Back in the Blue Land Ota stirred restlessly upon his multan, at the very moment when Iva called to him from the depths of the despair in her heart.

"For the second time I feel the thoughts of my Lady." He spoke softly.

Yet Noa heard. "Can you not be sure?" he asked.

"In my heart I am, but I can establish no clear contact here." Ota tapped his forehead. "I have sent out to her the message that I am coming, but I have no knowledge that she will receive it any more than I actually know she called to me. My Father's magic works well."

Noa made no response. Nothing he could say would ease the tortured mind of his Lord.

One tala or earth-day they had ridden steadily, stopping for nothing. Only one halt had been made in their furious ride. About the sixth hour after their start they had paused to rest the multans, for although the multans were strong beasts, much stronger than their earthly prototypes, yet every so often they must needs rest a little or they could not keep up their terrific pace.

When they took to the road again, they had covered the same distance in actual mileage that Efa had done in the long night.

Now they were nearing the Gates of Gecca—Ota's Gates. Soon, Noa knew, they would be able to see the glint of the Golden wall which surrounded Gecca. The Great Mind had protected his territory well, for he had had built for himself the Golden Wall that was the wonder of Venus.

At least thirty feet high and ten feet thick, the wall entirely encircled Gecca. There were only four entrances to it, one for each land. Each gateway, of heavy carved gold, was studded with the jewels of the ruler of the land to which entry was gained. Thus Ota's gate was rich in ornamentations of sapphires, while Leta's Gateway of the Red Land was garnished with rubies, Pra's with emeralds and Toa's with topazes. These gateways were in the side of the wall that touched the land of their owners, and they opened into a passage that ran through the ten foot thickness of the wall. Then on the other side was another gate which touched on the soil of Gecca and was guarded by the Great Mind's men. Thus making entrance to Gecca without the consent of the Great Mind practically an impossibility.

All this Noa knew well and as they drew nearer and nearer to the wall, he watched the lines in Ota's face grow more haggard and saw the pain deepen in his eyes.

Finally, unable to bear the sight of his friend's suffering, he turned to Gertrada. "There has been no sign anywhere of our Lord's Lady and the Messenger's passing?" he asked, but his words were more a statement than a question.

Gertrada shook her head sadly. "They did not pass this way."

Ota overheard. "I fear that you are right. We have traveled far but I have seen no trace, no tracks or sign of anything displaced. But soon—soon—we will reach the Gates of Gecca, and then—then we will know!"

Chapter XX
The Great Mind's Home

W hen they drew up before the Golden Gates, Iva caught her breath. Even in the midst of her terror she could not fail but gasp at the beauty of these golden portals gleaming with greenish tints of the emeralds which formed a fantastic pattern over their great surface.

Iva had seen all Europe—its beautiful cathedrals, even the most famous of carved doors which were Italy's pride, but never anywhere had she seen anything more lovely than the entrance to Gecca. She was so engrossed in the superb sight that she failed to hear the parley or note the yellow men who guarded the huge gates.

Presently she was brought back to her surroundings by a noise resembling the low rumble of thunder, which was the sound made by the gates as they swung open.

Almost before she had time to grasp what was happening, she was swept through them by her escort. The multans walked slowly the ten feet through the wall, which towered high above them on either side.

Ahead of her she could see another pair of gates. They were solid gold carved exquisitely but with no opening that she could discover. When they came very near to these gates, they halted and the man who had spoken to her in the forest called out, "The Great Mind's servants, bringing the Earth Girl, crave admission."

A tiny window opened and a face peered out. There was an exchange of names, then a voice called, "Enter, servants of the Great Mind, bringing the Earth Girl. The Great Mind receives you into his kingdom of Gecca."

Suddenly a door in the right-hand gate, about fifteen feet in height and five feet wide, swung open. It provided enough room for a multan and its rider to pass through. Apparently the huge thirty-foot gates of Gecca were not often opened.

Iva's heart sank. What chance would Ota have of passing through these inner gates? Even if they opened to him, they would never allow his army to pass. Truly Dante's lines should be en-graved over the portal of the door through which she was now passing: "Abandon Hope all ye who enter here." Dante's Inferno and the Great Mind's Gecca to Iva were one and the same.

As they waited for the last multan with its rider to come through, she heard the rumbling noise like thunder and knew Pra's gates were being shut.

Iva rode through the Golden City in a kind of daze. Every-where was gold glittering brightly in the rays of the Red Sun. It looked as though King Midas had touched each thing with his mag-ic finger, transmuting it to precious metal. The houses were built of gold, the streets were paved with bricks of it.

Here for the first time since her arrival on Venus, Iva saw chil-dren. Children were playing in the streets with golden toys, strange vari-colored creatures like the men who were escorting her. They stopped their play as Iva drew near and stood staring at her. Men and women came from their houses to get a closer view.

"I know now just how the elephant in a circus parade must feel," thought Iva.

She smiled at one little boy but he did not make a response to her advances. She made no second attempt, nor did she look at the houses which lined the broad avenue up which they were riding. They were all alike, these houses, square, massive things.

She could distinguish something far, far ahead, that towered high above everything. For a long time she could not make out what this was but she dimly suspected it must be the home of the Great Mind.

They rode on and on. Finally they came to a park which had an openwork fence around it, and gates, like iron grilles only in gold. Guards like the Messenger admitted them after the now familiar formula had been gone through.

"The Great Mind's servants, bringing the Earth Girl, crave admission."

Only in the reply was there a slight difference. "Enter, Servants of the Great Mind, bringing the Earth Girl. The Great Mind receives you into his home."

The Great Mind's home! As they rode through the park towards the towering edifice, Iva could see everything more plainly. She had thought Ota's Palace of the Four Towers magnificent. She had mentally compared that to Versailles. But this huge building did not invite comparison. It was beyond comprehension almost, and more beautiful and gorgeous than anything Iva had ever seen. She searched vainly in her mind for a comparison but finally gave up, for she could think of no earthly counterpart.

Like the Cathedral at Milan, this edifice was a mass of carving. But the delicate tracery in the gold was much more lace-like and lovely than the one she had thought the surpassing triumph of Man.

The Great Mind's home was about forty times larger than the Italian Cathedral, with a golden dome like St. Peter's in Rome. This was easily the size of Central Park, Iva decided. It was divided into four parts, each part being studded with the stone that represented one of its four lands, almost like a map of Venus.

The closer they came to the Palace, the more beautiful it grew. In gazing on this scene, Iva almost forgot that this was the home of the being she dreaded beyond all things—almost but not quite. The Great Mind was like the sword of Damocles, hanging over her head with the difference that she knew the blow would be upon her shortly.

They progressed up the broad avenue that led to the Palace. Iva noticed that while the grass was yellow, the trees were of the four different colors that Venus knew. The flowers also were vari-colored. This effect was less strange to Iva than the countries in one solid color had been.

Iva was trying to keep her mind on commonplace things and it was a desperate effort in this land where there was nothing that was not unusual.

As they drew nearer, more guards came out to meet them. Presently they halted beside a long flight of golden steps. The men leaped from their multans and their leader came and caught Iva as she slid down.

Without giving her time to remonstrate, he hurried her up the steps.

At the top two men were waiting with a chair arrangement. Swung about their broad shoulders on a sort of harness, the chair dangled empty between them. Into this Iva was helped. No sooner was she seated than they started towards the entrance to the Palace.

They moved so swiftly that all details were lost to Iva. She knew that they went through open doors into a long hall and then through numerous rooms. Before the entrance to each, the inevitable formula was gone through. The reply was the same until they came to the end. So Iva knew through what rooms she passed.

"The Great Mind receives you into his Hall,
"Into his Guard Room,
"Into his Blue Room,
"Into his Red Room,
"Into his Yellow Room,
"Into his Green Room,
"Into his First Antechamber,
"Into his Second Antechamber,
"Into his Waiting Room."

And finally the words that Iva had so dreaded fell heavily upon her ears:

"The Great Mind receives you into his Throne Room!"

Yet one more set of doors was thrown open and Iva was carried through.

She found herself in an enormous Audience Hall of gigantic proportions. The room was crowded with people, men and women, mostly the vari-colored inhabitants of Gecca, but among them were some Yellow, Red and Green people. Only of the Blue race was there no representative. Iva looked in vain for a tinge of the color that would mean help to her.

At the end of the Hall, which was far, far away, was a raised dais, upon which Iva could distinguish a figure seated in a golden chair. As they approached, she saw that the figure was covered entirely by a veil made of some glittering mesh, through which one could not possibly see anything but an outline.

When the foot of the dais was reached, the men escorting Iva fell to their faces on the floor, with the exception of the two carrying her, who remained erect.

The figure on the dais raised a hand beneath the veil. The men rose and their spokesman stepped forward.

"We have brought the Earth Girl according to thy commands, Oh, Master."

From under the veil came a voice, mellow and resonant, yet with some strange, unreal quality about it that clutched at Iva's heart like an icy hand. "You have done well and great shall be your reward. Let the Earth Girl come nearer."

Now Iva rose; clasping her arms across her breasts she walked to the edge of the dais.

"I demand," she began ...

Before she could finish, the voice she already hated interrupted her, "Bring the Earth Girl before my throne."

Two men sprang forward and each of them caught hold of one of Iva's wrists. She tried vainly to keep her arms in the position she had chosen, but she was no match for the men who half dragged her forward.

She did not scream. She realized the futility of any struggle only too well.

The voice was speaking, "Hold the Earth Girl firmly. The Great Mind wishes to look upon her."

Iva felt eyes sweeping over her, and despite herself she shrank back and hung her head. Each minute seemed an eternity of agony. If the Great Mind's voice alone repelled her, what would she do when she had to look into the eyes that pierced through her so burningly?

After a short while, the voice spoke again, "The Great Mind is pleased with the girl he summoned from the Earth planet. Take her to the women and make her ready for the eighth ga, for then the Great Mind will receive her in his inmost chamber."

While Iva bit her lips to keep from screaming, the veiled figure rose and with great deliberation took off the golden mesh covering which he laid reverently upon the carved throne. As he did so he spoke again, and curiously his voice was different. More soft and pleasing, it lacked entirely the uncanny quality that had so frightened Iva.

"I, Frathra, now put aside the mantle of the Great Mind and carry out my Master's commands to escort the Earth Girl to the women's quarters."

Iva caught her breath in a little sobbing gasp as the realization swept over her that she had yet to face the Great Mind.

Chapter XXI
Ruler of Venus

The time that passed before the eighth ga seemed like a dream to Iva. She followed Frathra and submitted to the ministrations of the Great Mind's women, hardly aware of what was happening.

She knew in some inmost corner of her mind that she created a sensation when she entered the women's quarters. She dimly noted the beauty of the large room to which they took her, but nothing registered very clearly in her mind.

She submitted to the hath they gave her in a sunken pool and made no objections to being rubbed with some sweet-scented oil that made her body glisten in the rosy light. She stood silently while they wrapped a length of vari-colored silk about her and said nothing when they combed out her soft golden curls.

A strange lethargy descended upon her. Nothing seemed to matter. The chattering of the women fell upon deaf ears. Only her heart kept crying, "Ota!" but there was no answer.

Eventually, when they had finished with her, she followed Frathra down interminable corridors lined with guards. If she had been noticing things, she would have realized that there was a martial atmosphere in the Great Mind's Palace. This would have been a comfort to her, but she did not try to associate ideas. The thing that she had dreaded was upon her, with no possible chance of escape, and she seemed frozen into a kind of numbness by the horror of the situation.

She wondered why she didn't think of her mother. People usually did under such circumstances. She then decided that Venus was responsible for the fact that all family affection had died within her. Already her earth body had adjusted itself to Venusian conditions, so her affections must have done the same, and she was like the inhabitants of the planet for only Ota mattered.

But even the thought of Ota's name failed to bring the usual thrill. Truly, she was like one walking in a sleep, impervious to anything.

Frathra came to a halt before a door which, though much smaller, was almost a duplicate of the entrance in the Golden Gates. The little window opened at their approach.

"Who comes?" the one corner of her brain which functioned heard.

"I, Frathra, bring the Earth Girl, according to your commands," was the response.

"Let the Earth Girl enter, alone!"

Iva came alive. This was the same voice she had heard issuing from Frathra's lips when he was representing the Great Mind, that same repellent, metallic tone, which now as then struck terror to her soul. It was a voice that might have issued from a python's throat, if snakes could speak. There was something slimy and reptilian about it.

Iva drew nearer to Frathra.

A door, just big enough for Iva to pass through without bending, swung open.

The girl, in utter panic, caught Frathra's great hand in both of hers. "Save me," she cried softly, "By the Red Sun which you worship, I beg you to save me!"

The vari-colored man's eyes looked at her pityingly, but no hint of sympathy was in his voice as he said, "You must not keep the Ruler of Venus waiting."

Then he shook off her appealing hands and taking her by the shoulders, pushed her gently but firmly through the door.

Iva heard the door shut behind her. There was an air of finality about the way it clanged to.

"Come closer," the voice commanded her.

Despite herself, Iva moved forward, her eyes upon the ground. She did not dare raise them for the overwhelming certainty swept over her that she was alone with the Great Mind, the Ruler of Venus!

For several seconds there was a silence. Then the voice spoke again.

"You are truly beautiful! Look at me."

Iva raised her eyes. She let them pass idly over the room before she obeyed the instructions. Somehow, she wanted to put off the evil moment as long as she could.

The room was large and square, with golden walls that had no transparent sides such as there had been in the Blue Palace. There were several chests, a throne chair, and against the wall at her right a huge couch, upon which, half reclining and half sitting among luxurious cushions, was a man. Knowing that the moment could be put off no longer, for the first time she looked squarely at the Great Mind.

Iva gasped with amazement. She was not quite sure what she had expected to see, but she had been prepared for some monstrosity. Instead, regarding her with cold steel-grey eyes, was perhaps the most handsome man she had ever seen. The Great Mind was beautiful—beautiful as a statue is beautiful, cold and unearthly.

Tall and slim, his skin was rose. With his red hair forming little curls about his forehead he looked like Michelangelo's statue of David, tinted. His lips were full and thick. His face was quite expressionless as he looked at Iva.

Just so must Satan look, the girl decided—Satan as he waited to consign a victim to Hell's fires. So might Medusa have appeared to those whom her glance turned into stone—beautiful, with an evil beauty that struck terror into the hearts of all who saw. Such was the Great Mind.

He stretched out one perfectly proportioned hand to Iva. "Come closer," he said.

Iva shuddered. She would just as soon coil a snake about her fingers as touch that hand. Beautiful as he might be, the Great Mind inspired her with a horror and loathing beyond description.

She remembered once having been taken to an aquarium when she was a child. In a tank had been an octopus. She had given it one look and run screaming away. But she had never forgotten the sinking feeling in the pit of her stomach the sight of the repulsive thing had given her.

That same feeling she was experiencing now, but she could not run away, and screaming would do her no good. Some innate sense told her that if she evinced terror, the being watching her would enjoy it. She could not think of the Great Mind as a man. He was too unnatural to be classed with other people.

He leaned forward and caught her wrist. Slowly, inexorably he drew her closer, closer. Iva tried to struggle. His clasp was like iron, irresistible. When she realized this, Iva screamed.

For the first time he smiled. "Again, my beautiful. That is music to my ears. Not for centuries have my caresses met with resistance. Truly, I did well to call you to me from your home on Earth."

No matter what happened, Iva decided she would not scream again. This creature must be a sadist, and he should at least lack that much satisfaction.

One look into his steel-blue eyes had convinced her that an appeal to his mercy would go unanswered; yet she felt it must be made.

Ignoring his caresses, she spoke. "My Lord, Ruler of Venus, I belong to your son!"

In the same even, metallic tone that filled her with aversion, he replied. "You wear his belt and head-piece, but you are not yet his. Fool that he was!" The full red lips curved a little into a smile that was really a snarl. "Fool, not to drink deep of the cup so near at hand! He waited to take you to the Temple, a virgin, to be his by our laws. Well, his loss is my gain, for he will not be able to take you to the Temple after this hour. For his folly I will have a little mercy when I deliver judgment upon him."

From his tone Iva knew that there would be no mercy for the man she loved, and in the midst of her distress she prayed Ota would not come.

Though she knew it was useless, Iva made one more struggle. "I hate you as much as I love Ota. Surely you wouldn't want a woman who hated you!"

Now the ruler of Venus smiled, and his smile suggested unutterable things. "I want once again to drink deep of passion. Do you think I care whether you love or hate me? Does the fact that you hate me make your lips less sweet? No, no, my beautiful, it only makes me want you more!"

His face came nearer, towards her. Iva knew now there was no hope. In one second those full sensuous lips would touch hers—and then—.

Perhaps when he tired of her he would let her die—that would be all that could be left for her—death and forgetfulness!

"Ota," she breathed despairingly, as the Great Mind pressed his lips to hers.

Chapter XXII
Ota's Gate

As they drew nearer to the Golden Gates, Noa's heart ached more and more for his master.

When they first sighted the blue blaze which came from the sapphires set in the doors, Noa marked the circles under the Blue Lord's eyes, which had grown deeper as they rode along and there was no sign of Iva.

Ota said nothing, but as he gave his multan the signal to stop, the lines of his handsome face were etched with grief. His first words to the guards who rushed forward to greet him were, "Have you heard or seen aught of My Lady?"

The arms of the guards uplifted in salutation, fell. Their leader, or Captain, spoke. "She has not passed these portals, Lord. A messenger from Pra awaits you."

Ota answered and there was a catch in his voice at the confirmation of his fears, "Bid the messenger from the Yellow Lord step forth."

Behind Ota in a little close ring was Noa, Gerlrada, and the rest of Ula's sons with their wives. Then there was a little clear space, and beyond that stretched Ota's following—thousands of Blue men and women on their multans, who all stood quietly waiting for a word from their Lord.

From the center of a small group of guards, the Captain brought a Green Man forward towards Ota. The man raised his right arm in salutation and at a sign from Ota moved close, waiting for permission to speak, which the Blue Lord was not long in giving.

The Green Man began hesitatingly. "I bear a message; my Master has heard you can bind thoughts."

Ota understood. There was utter silence while he gazed concentratedly into the Green Man's eyes.

No one heard the softly murmured words he spoke. After a little while he raised his voice, "You can now speak safely, though of a truth if my father's thoughts are not elsewhere he has already read your message."

Even Ota did not guess that at that moment the Great Mind was so occupied with Iva that for once he had no interest in the thoughts of others, and any conversation they had would have been safe.

"My Lord Pra," the Green Man was saying, "says to tell you that in the ensuing war he and the Lords of the Red and Yellow Lands will remain neutral—they will give no help to the Ruler of Venus against you, as by rights they should, if you will confirm them in the possession of their kingdoms should you be victorious."

For the first time since Iva's disappearance, a faint smile showed on Ota's lips.

"And if I lose? How would they make their peace with the Great Mind?"

The Green Messenger answered promptly, "The men will be delayed on their march, Lord Ota. Already at the Great Mind's command they have started to close in upon the rear of your army. But if they meet, perchance, the Fiery Beasts and have to change their route, there is no blame, and in the stress of battle perhaps the Great Mind will not know truth. Besides, we do not think that you will lose."

Noa put his hand on Ota's wrist. "This is indeed tribute, my Lord."

"Tribute founded on the hope of a people that weary of my Father's tyranny," Ota said softly into Noa's ear. "Besides, I remember once a daughter of Pra's, a girl he loved that my Father took into his household—there was a tale—."

The Messenger continued, "Furthermore, Lord Pra said that if you agreed to his terms, he had news for you that your ears burn to hear."

Now Ota was on the alert and his fine resonant voice rang out, "If I triumph, Pra, Leta and Toa will continue to rule their kingdoms; furthermore, they will have more power than they have ever had before. My word is given in the presence of my people; and I also promise if I lose that the Ruler of Venus will know naught of these negotiations through me or my people. Now, man, your news!"

Ota leaned down with his head almost level with the multan's mane and his eyes fixed on those of the Messenger.

Seeing the hope that shone forth from the Blue Lord's eyes, the Green Man hung his head, for he knew his news would wipe away that light.

"Some thirty or more of the Great Mind's guards took the Earth Girl through Pra's Gates into Gecca."

Ota's face was like a slate over which a sponge had passed wiping all the writing away. No expression of any kind remained on the Blue Lord's features. Perfectly chiseled they stood forth, firm and unbetraying—only his eyes were pits of misery.

In a voice which gave no hint of the agony he was suffering, he asked, "At what ga?"

The Green man answered, "Four gas ago, Lord Ota."

Noa knew just what his Master was thinking. Iva had been four hours in Gecca; long enough in the Golden Palace to spell ruin to Ota's hopes, even allowing for the time taken to reach the Great Mind's home through the outlying territory of Gecca, which in itself was such a journey that only the swift-footed multans could traverse it quickly. For a man on foot to go from the Golden Gates to the Palace would take at least an Earth week, whereas the multans could do it in about three gas.

It was now sometime after the eighth ga. Even if Iva had not been taken at once to the Great Mind long before they could reach the Palace, it would be too late. If Ota could force the gates, they might by exerting the multans to their utmost, reach the Palace in two gas; but fighting would be encountered on the way, constant delays.

So far as Noa could see there was no hope.

He looked up and met Ota's eyes. Through the despair which registered so plainly, blazed a new force. As though he had followed Noa's thoughts, Ota said.

"At least, we will have revenge."

Noa's hand clasped Ota's wrist. "To the end!" he said. "I am your man!"

"When I find my Lady, I will make a new law and she will yet be my wife," Ota went on.

Now Noa gasped, for in all of Venus such a thing had never happened. When a woman belonged to a man she was his forever. There was no promiscuity on Venus.

"We waste time, and time is precious," Ota said. In his voice was no hope, only a desperateness. "Go back to the Yellow Lord and tell him my words," he told the Green Messenger.

The guards of the Gate brought forward a multan with a green band upon its forehead. Without further parley the Messenger leaped upon its back and rode off through the ranks of Ota's followers who opened up their solid formation to let him pass.

Now Ota spoke tersely to the guards who watched the Gates. "Open!"

The huge gates swung apart.

Ota turned to Noa. "Go you ahead. Demand entrance in my name."

Noa rode down the narrow passage. When he reached the second Gates he followed the same procedure that the guards escorting Iva had used.

The little window in the tall Golden Gates opened. Behind it appeared the head of one of the Great Mind's men. "Who comes?" he asked.

"Lord Ota demands admittance into Gecca with his following," Noa responded firmly.

"The Gates of Gecca are closed to the Blue People. My Master says that his son, the Lord Ota of the Blue Land, may enter unescorted and face his trial for disobedience." The vari-colored man rolled out his words in a parrot-like fashion.

Noa responded, "I will carry your words to My Lord."

"I will await your Lord's reply."

Noa went back to Ota to whom he repeated what the man had said.

Throwing his head back, Ota laughed long and loud. "Go back again, my friend, and say that Ota and his people will enter into Gecca before a quarter of a ga is passed."

With wonder in his heart, Noa obeyed.

The man on the other side of the window smiled as he finished. "These gates are strong," he said. "We do not fear. Even should your Master pass their portals, he would find a welcome that he would not expect." And the window clanged shut, ominously, Noa thought.

He went back to Ota and repeated what he had heard.

Ota, turning, addressed his people. "Now is our moment. We dare not wait. After we pass the Gates, we will find my Father's army waiting for us. They, as you know, are armed with our usual fighting-gear—the stick that burns. You know also, that unless the burn is very deep, it heals in time. But the sheaths you carry are a new weapon. They send forth a fire that consumes and casts into oblivion all it touches. Only, you must handle your weapon carefully. Hold it so."

Ota took the long tube from his belt and held it with his two hands projecting forth from the level of his waist.

"Not one inch higher or lower is safe. When you slip back the shield that covers the end, a ray comes forth that focused upon a human being reduces that person to ashes. The apron you wear protects you from the reflection.

"You must only open the shield when an enemy is in front of you, and when he is annihilated you press a button you will find on the side and the shield slides back into place. Aim the tube at the middle of your opponent, the rays spread. Do you understand?"

With one voice the multitude answered, "Yes!"

Ota continued, "When we get through the Gate, spread yourselves in a straight line. Keep on enlarging it, for the ones in the rear are useless, as they must not unsheath their tubes."

"We hear and we obey," shouted the people.

"One last word. The women wait in the rear, ready to come forth, if necessary."

Gertrada and Erda shook their heads. A look passed between them. Each knew that the other would be in the first line of the advancement.

There was a sudden hush. Each person held the tube as Ota had shown, with one finger near the button, another touching the little handle that would release the shield that covered the deadly ray.

Ota swung back facing the narrow passage to the Golden Gates. "Follow me!" he cried out as he gave his multan the signal to start.

Chapter XXIII
The Choice

Iva's sensations, when she first felt the Great Mind's lips descend upon hers, were indescribable. Held so firmly that to move was an impossibility, she had no way of preventing the caress that filled her with horror.

For one sickening second she thought she was going to faint but she made a heroic effort to keep herself from sinking into oblivion, for at the first touch of those thick velvety lips she had resolved to fight!

Suddenly the Great Mind released Iva, as a strange look spread over his face. He seemed entirely unconscious of her presence.

For several minutes he stood there, rigid, almost as though he were in a trance. Then just as suddenly, he became himself again. He put one arm under her shoulders and drew her close. He caressed her gently while he whispered in her ear.

"See, I will not frighten you—no, I will only beg you to be kind to me. For years, centuries, even before you were born, I have waited for this moment, waited and longed for the time when again I would know the thrills that once were mine. On all of Venus there is no nature so passionate as mine. My subjects are faithful. They are happy with their wives and slaves. A new slave every century keeps them content. So they conserve their vital force. But I—I need love! No one woman—no hundred slave-girls—could content my passions!"

He raised himself on one elbow and looked down at her. "Did you not know that great mental activity requires great stimulation?"

Iva shook her head. Not for worlds would she have interrupted the flow of his conversation.

"I have made Venus, its laws, its countries and its people. From a wild place populated with savages, I—a savage—have built up a civilization. In the beginning there were only the secrets of what had gone before—in the age that was past. I, alone of all the remnants that were left, had the brain to delve into the knowledge of those who had gone, and from them to found a new age and build up the civilization that you see."

"Like father, like son," thought Iva. "They both learned their wisdom from the ancients."

The Great Mind went on: "But to do all that, I needed stimulation for my mind, and I found it only in the senses. So I spent notoriously of my passion, not realizing that the day would come when nothing would be left to spend. See, I am gentle and I am pleading with you. Give me back what I have lost, if only for one hour. I, the Great Mind, Ruler of Venus, beg—I, who command, implore!"

Almost, Iva was sorry for this cold, arrogant creature, who was abasing himself before her; almost she pitied him, but her hatred was stronger than her pity.

Before her was personified the material, the sensuous—a being who thought of nothing but the flesh-pots of life. No wonder he filled her with loathing.

Without moving from his arms, or looking at him, she gave her answer. "I love your son. To him only will I give myself."

The gentleness of which he had made so much, dropped from the Great Mind. He threw it off as he would a mantle, and in its place came something new—not the coldness with which he had first greeted Iva, but a concentrated fury and determination that was almost maniacal in its intensity.

"You will do what I ask—or I will send you back to Earth!"

Despair leaped into Iva's eyes, despite her efforts to maintain a calm. Never to see Ota again! To return to the life that was so far behind her it seemed almost as though it never had been! To take up a Twentieth Century existence after knowing the wonders of Venus and Ota's love! This seemed impossible, but at least her love for Ota and his for her would be unsoiled, unsullied. She would go back to earth and spend the rest of her life longing for the Blue Lord.

For once the great mind read her thoughts. "Before I send you back to your Earth, I will let my guards show you what you deprive me of. Then I shall have a tale to tell my son of what happened to his chosen Lady before I returned her to her home."

For one second he ceased speaking, then he went on and his voice was like an acid which burns away everything it touches.

"Shall I call my men to amuse you while I get ready to send you back to Earth? Or will you be kind to me? Come, which is it to be? Choose."

Chapter XXIV
The Deadly Ray

Ota rode down the narrow passage closely followed by Noa and the rest of Ula's sons. When he came quite near to the door he paused.

"Are you ready?" he asked Noa.

"Quite, My Lord. I hold my tube firmly against me."

"Pass the word back that our multans must keep their heads low when we unsheathe our weapons." Ota bent over and whispered a few words to his mount. The great beast understood and whinnied softly.

"Stand ready to come forward!" Ota cried and pulled back the protective cap from the end of his tube. A strange blue light emanated from the long narrow object. Its rays touched the Golden Door. Before their eyes the door dissolved into nothing.

For one second Noa saw through the gaping space. Line after line of the Great Mind's guards were standing behind a long, curious-looking bar. Then the ray touched them and they, too, dissolved into nothingness. The bar, which such a short time before had looked so solid and substantial, was no longer there.

Ota moved forward, his weapon still held in front of him, wreaking destruction. The Blue Ray passed over the multan's head harmlessly, to bring annihilation to the advancing guards.

The Great Mind's soldiers were crowding into the space left by the disappearance of their comrades, not quite understanding what had happened.

Noa advanced to Ota's side and unsheathed his tube, holding it as he had been taught. He leaned his body to the right so he would not conflict with Ota.

Gotha swung himself into position at Ota's left, and yet another beam of blue light added to the havoc.

The others gradually came inside the wall through the large entrance, the massive doors, now missing, had left. As Ota and his companions moved forward, they spread themselves along the wall with their weapons unsheathed. They, too, brought destruction to the guardians of Gecca.

The first line was entirely demolished. The second line of men, beginning dimly to understand what was happening, kept back out of reach of the deadly ray, which did not throw its emanations a great distance. The one Ota held reached farther than any other.

So far, although perhaps a thousand of the Great Mind's men were extinct, there had been no noise. The very silence was uncanny. Ota's followers were too intent on obeying their Lord's instructions and too awestruck at the workings of their new weapons, to make outcry—and their opponents were too horror-stricken.

Noa expected his Master to give the signal to advance at any moment. Obviously, all that was necessary was for them to move a little closer to the opposing army. Instead, he was struck with amazement to see Ota press the button that put the protective shield back into place over his weapon. He watched wonderingly to see what would happen next.

Ota raised himself on his multan and called out loudly, his rich voice quite filling the gap between the two armies. "I do not wish to slaughter unnecessarily—to send men to oblivion if I can avoid it. You have seen how easily I can advance through you. Will you surrender?"

Now a man stepped forward. He held up his right arm. "Can I come closer?" he called.

Ota bade him come and turning to Noa he said loudly, "Sheathe your weapons but be ready to let them work again at the first sign of movement from the opposing forces."

By this time the man who had spoken had ridden forward. He came so near that the heads of the multans almost met.

"Greetings, Lord Ota, Ruler of the Blue Land. I am Gana," he said simply.

Ota responded to his salutation. "You were once of my household when I lived in Gecca. I remember you well."

"I am honored, my Lord. We have obeyed the commands of our Master, the Great Mind, and, lo!—thousands of us have vanished into space! Will they return?"

Sadly Ota shook his head. "There are not even ashes left, Gana. The blue ray is powerful."

"A deadly weapon, Lord," responded the man, shrinking back a little from the tube-weapon. "The rest of us do not wish to feel its force. We have no desire to leave Venus. If we become your men, will you protect us from the Great Mind's wrath, you, who are all-powerful?"

"You shall be as my own people," Ota told him and raised his voice so all could hear. "Nor is there any blame to you in this, nor reflection on your honor as fighting-men."

"Then we surrender." Gana turned and addressed the waiting thousands. "From the lips of the Blue Lord you have heard his promise. Will you join with him?"

"We will," came from thousands of throats.

Gana turned back. "And we thank you for your mercy," he added.

The Blue Lord smiled, then said, "Have your men pile their sticks that burn, on the ground before me."

Gana gave the order and one by one the men filed by, laying their sticks upon the ground. Before many minutes had elapsed, a small mountain of them had grown up in front of the Blue Lord.

While they were thus engaged, Ota put a question to Gana. "Did my Father not have some preparation made to receive us?"

A noticeable gleam of humor showed in Gana's eyes as he replied. "The Great Mind had built a barrier. Whoever touched it would have been burned beyond healing. It was so placed that anyone entering from the gates could not have failed to contact with it—it went with the gates."

"Do you know of what it was made?"

"It contained the same material that is used for our sticks, Lord, but of greater quantity."

"Are there more of such bars in Gecca?"

"No, Lord, it was not thought necessary."

Now the men signaled to Gana that all their weapons had been placed in front of the Blue Lord.

Ota called out, "Stand back, all!" and told Gana to wheel his multan alongside of his.

When the erstwhile leader of the Great Mind's forces had obeyed, Ota took his tube and releasing the guard, turned the deadly ray upon the pile of sticks. As its blue light touched the small mountain, a murmur of astonishment arose, for in less space than it takes a man to draw his breath, the mountain was gone. No sign of the weapons remained, not even so much as a single ash.

Ota turned again to Gana. "Are more troops about?"

"At each gate, and guarding the Palace, my Lord."

"Then send men to tell them and ask for their surrender to each of the Gates. Tell them if they become my men, I confirm all their rights, but if not I will reduce Gecca to a barren plain where no thing breathes. I will send some of my men with you in case they need a demonstration of how my ray works. Let other men attend to the rebuilding of this Gate. I would not have the uniformity of the Golden Walls disturbed. You and the remainder of your men ride with me to the Palace."

Ota signaled to Ula's sons to divide themselves into Captains and go with the vari-colored men. Only Noa and Gotha he kept with him.

Gana gave terse orders and three detachments of men rode off in different directions to the other gates. Then Gana returned to the Blue Lord saying, "Your commands have been obeyed."

"You will ride ahead with your men and explain as you go. I do not wish to have to wreak more destruction. Go fast, Gana, for I have much to do when I reach the Palace." Ota's voice trembled.

Gana set off followed by hundreds of the vari-colored men.

With sad eyes that showed no gleam of joy in his victory, Ota spoke gently to Gotha. "Go, tell the people in the rear who have not yet entered the Gates, what has transpired, and that they can put their weapons back into their belts. We will need them no more. We ride swiftly—they can follow at their ease."

Gotha departed as Noa rode up. Close beside his Master, he cried triumphantly, "Gecca is yours!" He continued, "And not even a quarter of your army inside the walls!"

"Gecca is mine, and my way clear to the Palace. But do not forget, oh, my friend, that inside that Palace is the Great Mind and my Lady!"

There was a pause, then Ota's deep, melodious voice throbbed out, as the lower notes of a harp might have done, "And by the Red Sun, I would lose ten thousand Geccas rather than arrive there too late!"

Chapter XXV
Efa

While all these events were taking place, Efa was riding like mad over the Blue Lands towards Gecca.

True to the plans she had made as the Messenger and Iva vanished in the distance, she had trudged doggedly in the direction where she thought the nearest cluta, or town, would be.

As she walked over the soft blue grass, she crooned to herself, playing with words until eventually from vague sentences grew a song. She was pleased with her efforts and she sang it over and over.

"Her skin is like the soft flush of the rising sun,

"Her hair reflects the gold of the Topaze stone.

"Her eyes are bluer than the Blue Land—

"She is all beautiful!

"Her beauty is a beauty that tears the heart;

"It has torn my heart from my bosom

"And nothing but love of her has a place therein.

"She is all beautiful!

"Because she scorned me and my affection,

"Because she loved another and not me,

"Because she deserted me without regret,

"She shall know my revenge!"

She repeated this over and over, but finally she left off the first two verses and only sang the last.

The more she sang, the more intense she grew, and the more her already fevered brain became excited. By the time she reached the outlying houses of the cluta, she could think of nothing but her revenge and the nearest way to it.

At the moment, the one thing she wanted most was a multan, a multan that would take her swiftly to her revenge. Just how she was going to accomplish her desire was beyond her. She, herself, was perfectly safe, as her invisibility protected her. The multan, however, would be visible to all eyes.

Once she got the animal out of the stable, it would appear as though the beast were running off. That in itself would be a rare thing on Venus, where the multans were not only mounts, but friends. Besides, it was highly conceivable, unless she could find some plausible reason, that the multan might refuse to leave its stall.

Indeed, this was a problem that might have puzzled a better brain than Efa's, but with the cunning ingenuity of an unsound mind, she set about solving the puzzle.

First she walked around the houses that were separate from the town, to see whether they were occupied, for in Venus each head of a family owns two houses, or dwelling-places—one in the town and another in what would correspond to the country on Earth. Only the Venusians generally had their country places on the outskirts of the cluta wherein they lived, to make the going back and forth easier.

Efa knew that in the town houses she would not have much chance of annexing a steed for herself, as the multans were kept in one of the lower wings of the house; but outside the Cluta the multans generally had a separate building of their own, not far from the house, it is true—because the Venusians and their multans were never very far apart as the people could go nowhere without their swift steeds. The distance on Venus being so great, they were absolutely dependent on their multans for transportation.

Picking out the largest of the country homes, Efa walked into it with the assurance that she could not be seen.

Like all the Venusian houses, this one was in three stories; the first floor being one huge room where the entire family gathered together, while the upper stories contained suites of sleeping rooms. The country houses were large and spacious because they were used by the entire family with all its various branches and ramifications, whereas in the towns the houses were smaller, as each had his own dwelling-place, only the unmarried sons and daughters living with their parents.

Efa was lucky, for in the house she entered the entire family was gathered at the noonday meal. She moved nearer and stood behind the chair of one of the men. She listened carefully to the conversation but gleaned nothing from it of interest, for they were talking of family affairs. Quite evidently, no news of events at Gecca had reached them.

Efa's luck held, for shortly a man at the end of the long table broke in with something that did interest her.

"I brought home a new multan from the hatching ponds. It is of a size for my youngest child. I had it put into the stall next to Walda, who will watch its growth. I have named the animal 'Ga' because it will go more swiftly than the hour when it is full-grown."

"You have done well, Fadra, my son," came from a sweet-faced woman in reply.

Efa waited to hear no more. She ran lightly through the house and towards the stables. Nothing could better have suited her purpose, everyone being safely housed in the large room, too busy with their food to even look through the transparent wall.

Now that she knew the name of a multan, securing it would be easy. She went into the stable through the open door. "Walda," she called gently.

A huge multan came out of her stall, head arched, looking for the one who had called her.

Running behind the horse, Efa leaped upon its back with an agile hound. Then she leaned forwards and said softly into the animal's ear, "Fadra commands you take me to the Blue Gates of Gecca as quickly as possible, and that you stop for nothing."

The multan did not turn her head. She felt the weight of Efa's body and heard a command from her Master.

She tossed her mane and neighed loudly, which filled Efa's heart with fear that some of the people in the house might hear. Her fears were unfounded. No one came, and the multan, Walda, started forth in the direction of Ota's gates, at a terrific speed.

Once started on her way to Gecca, Efa went back to her song.

"Because she scorned me and my affection,

"Because she loved another and not me,

"Because she deserted me without regret,

"She shall know my revenge!"

She crooned it in a sing-song voice, too low for the multan to hear even if Walda could have understood. For the words the multans understand are limited. Efa, pleased with her idea of vengeance, was not going to share it with anyone beforehand.

Like Ota, she thought that of course the Messenger would take Iva to the Blue Gate.

After a while she got tired of repeating all four lines, so she limited herself to the last,

"She shall know my revenge!"

She tried other words in the place of "know"—

"She shall *see* my revenge!"

"She shall *feel* my revenge!"

"She shall *taste* my revenge!"

but she decided she liked the original version best, and sang it over and over to herself in a way that portended no good for the Earth Girl if they ever met. At length she got down to just the one word.

"Revenge!"

She mumbled it with her shriveled lips. Each beat of the multan's feet as they pounded on the turf, threw the word up to her. She saw it in crimson letters dancing before her eyes, until suddenly there seemed to be nothing else in the world,

"Revenge! REVENGE! R E V E N G E ! !"

She was so occupied with her thoughts that she failed to see the glitter of the Golden Wall in the distance. Her plans of what she would do to Iva once the Earth Girl was in her power again, kept her from noticing what was before her.

Not until she was within several yards of the vanguard of Ota's army was she conscious of her surroundings, and even then she would not have been distracted had not Walda, seeing other multans not very far away, neighed loudly, although she did not diminish her speed.

The sound of the horse brought Efa back to the practical side of the revenge that was all-important to her. In one horror-stricken instant she took in the Golden Walls with the huge gap made by the missing gates, and the fact that they were entirely surrounded by Blue Men who stretched far back over the Blue Land.

Frantic, she ordered the multan to go another direction. The multan paid no attention to Efa's commands. Her Master's words, as given to her, had been to go to the Blue Gates as quickly as possible, so without slackening her speed in the least degree, she thundered on.

"Walda, Walda!" cried Efa, "Turn back, turn back!"

Not a break was made in the furious pace. Now the apparently riderless horse was seen by one of the Blue People. Several of them turned and seeing the frightful rate of speed at which the steed was traveling, broke their ranks to let the animal through.

Walda rushed by them until she came to where Ota's sapphire-studded gates were thrown back, and then with a suddenness that almost unseated Efa, she stopped.

The Blue People crowded around the multan, so close that for Efa to slip off of Walda's back was impossible. One man, putting out his hand to stroke the mare's sleek side, touched Efa's foot. Despite his astonishment, he clung fast to it.

"There is someone on the multan!" he cried. "I can feel a human foot though I see nothing." He began moving his other hand upwards.

Efa saw that the game was up so far as her remaining undiscovered was concerned. She spoke the word that removed the mantle of invisibility from her body.

A low murmur of awe swept through the crowd as Efa appeared before them. The man let go his hold upon her foot in utter astonishment.

"Efa!" he cried.

"Efa," she replied, half mockingly. Then quite serious, "What happens here?"

"Lord Ota has taken Gecca. He is now on his way to the Palace to face the Great Mind," she was told.

"And his Lady?" How Gecca had been captured, mattered not to Efa, but for news of Iva her whole body waited-waited with the word "revenge" hanging before her eyes as though it had been wrought by fire.

The man was only too eager to give information. "The Lady, Iva, is in the Great Mind's Palace. We are all praying to the Red Sun that Lord Ota be not too late to save her."

Efa waited to hear no more. She looked at the man and waved her hand. "I bear news of the utmost importance. Take me to Lord Ota—at once—wherever he may be!"

And as they obeyed her commands, she laughed shrilly to herself, for now she knew that her revenge would not be far off.

Chapter XXVI
Lesser of Two Evils

While the Great Mind's "Choose" was still ringing in her ears, Iva decided that the only thing to do was to play for time. Ota, she was sure, must be coming. If she could succeed in keeping the Great Mind distracted sufficiently long to give Ota a chance to reach her, there might yet be hope—a forlorn hope, perhaps, but at any rate it was something to cling to—and between the two ways open to her it was the only road her feet could tread.

Therefore, when the Ruler of Venus cried, "Choose!" again, she answered him slowly yet deliberately, "You have given me no choice."

"You mean?"

"I mean one, no matter how abhorrent, is better than many."

The Great Mind smiled sardonically. "You do not flatter me."

"I cry a bargain," she went on, "If I yield and give you again the thrill you once knew, by my earth magic, you must agree to my conditions."

"I make conditions. I do not need to grant them."

"But these you must in order to attain your desire. Truly, I must be humored, Lord of Venus."

With an impatient shrug of his beautifully proportioned shoulders, he looked at her. In his eyes she read a frustrated longing so overpowering that she knew he would grant any demand within reason. Therefore his words did not surprise her. "It can do me no harm to hear your bargain."

"You must not hurry me. I need time to work my spells. There are questions I would ask." As she saw an expression of impatience

130

cross his face, she hurried on, "Questions about things on your Planet that puzzle me. Also you must promise me that after—."

He held up his hand, "I make no promises. After all, it is I who should dictate, not you. I have listened to you, but remember, I can force many things upon you if you do not accede to my demands. Time I have given you. The future is mine and depends entirely on how you please me. But I will answer two questions, and then—then I shall expect you to show me how Earth women love!"

The Great Mind had spoken truly. She was utterly helpless and in his power. What would happen to her if she failed, she did not like to think; and if she succeeded the outlook was equally bad. She was indeed between the "Devil and the blue sea." Only Ota could cause the black swirling waters that were enveloping her to fall back on either side and carry her safely through.

"Ota, Ota, come quickly!" she prayed in the inmost recesses of her mind. But there was no answer.

At least she had gained a little time. Two questions! She must ask something that would take long to answer. What could she ask?

The Great Mind's voice broke in upon her. "Well, my beautiful, I said two questions, but I did not say I would wait forever to have you put them to me."

Iva seized on the first thing she could think of. "I do not understand your stellar system. I'm not familiar with our Earth astronomy, but I think we credit Venus with having several moons."

"On Earth you see what we of the other planets wish you to see. Do you suppose for one instant we want you to know the truth about us? Not so! We cloud your vision so you cannot tell, or perhaps someone less stupid than the rest might find the way to reach us."

"But I am here."

"Because I brought you, and you are not a scientist who could bring hurt upon us, perhaps even set up a rivalry to my rule! You were brought for one purpose, and it is time that purpose was fulfilled." He caught her closely to him.

"Two questions—you promised me two questions!" Iva panted.

"Then be quick."

"Tell me—" she began, but just at that moment he released her entirely and sprang to his feet. In a perfect fury he stamped upon the floor. Then again that strange rigidity that he had displayed once before came over him.

Had Iva but known what he was seeing, her heart would have rejoiced. The first time he had gone into more or less of a trance, it had been to see Noa knocking at his Golden Gate. That had not disturbed him, nor had he even bothered to watch further, for he had had perfect faith in his burning-bar.

Just before Iva began to ask her second question, he had thrown his mind back to the gates and had seen his men reduced to nothing by the deadly blue ray his son wielded. Now in an inward rage he listened to the conversation between Ota and Gana and saw Gana ride off closely followed by Ota.

He knew that in desperation Ota would cover the ground to the Palace very quickly. He, himself, had made no further plans for the protection of his home, as he had been quite sure Ota would never pass the burning-bars.

Now, with his clear cold reasoning, he saw that there was little or nothing he could do. His men would join against him once they knew the situation and without time he could do nothing to combat the new weapon.

He admitted to himself, honestly enough, that even with time the deadly ray would be more than he could cope with.

His guards within the Palace were useless under these new conditions, for if his men did remain faithful to him, they would soon be sent to oblivion, and locking doors would be of no avail when the whole structure could be so easily dissolved.

The Ruler of Venus faced the fact that his rule was almost over. He could not even bargain with Ota, for he, too, could be consumed by the deadly ray.

For one instant the Great Mind regretted the past. Once he had had the love of his people, and he might have kept it. But he well knew that now he had only their hatred. Even on Venus where family affection was not strong, fathers and mothers resented the fall of their daughters.

If he had left the Earth Girl on her planet, Ota would not have risen against him. And on all Venus was no one else who could have accomplished such havoc.

The Earth Girl! He might bargain with his son over Iva. He could return her unharmed in exchange for reinstatement in his kingdom!

Almost as quickly as the idea entered his mind, he threw it forth.

To the second where he had been first; to rely on someone's mercy! There was a kind of nobility in his rejection of such a fate.

No, the Earth Girl was his and he would rob Ota of the thing he loved best! He, himself, would have the pleasures he anticipated, added to the joy of cheating Ota of all the triumph of his victory!

Even without having overheard Ota's own words, he would have known that without saving Iva all glory would he like ashes to his son.

He would love once more, then have his revenge, telling Ota he had come too late. And after that—the deadly ray or the fiery pit! It mattered not.

There was yet one more thing that he could do, not to save himself, but to gain time.

He threw his thoughts to Frathra, with whom he could always get into instant communication.

"When my Son, Lord Ota of the Blue Land, comes," he told his representative, "meet him on the steps and greet him for me. Then tell him I have retired to my secret chamber with the Earth Girl and that when I am ready, and not before, I will come forth to greet him. Also say that he cannot hope to find us. Even if he should demolish my Palace, which he would not be foolish enough to do, it would not avail him, for thus he would put an end forever to his erstwhile Lady."

Then the Great Mind told Frathra to repeat the message, and Frathra went over it word for word.

With the further admonition to say just that and no more, "For I will not this time be speaking through you as is my wont," the Ruler of Venus finished what might very well be his last command.

While all this was going on inside his brain, Iva, seeing he was so wrapt up in thought that he was oblivious of her, rose quietly from the couch.

Perceiving that she was unobserved, she made her way toward the door, hoping perhaps she might slip away. But when she looked, she could find no indication of an entrance of any kind. The Golden Walls were to all appearances unbroken. Even though she knew about where she had entered, Iva could not discover a trace of the door through which she had passed.

She did not give up until she had gone over every inch of wall space the room contained. Then she returned to the couch, prey to the utmost despair. She had made every effort of which she was capable. Truly, she was caught in a web from which there was no escape.

His low laugh brought her attention to the Great Mind.

"I am sorry to have left you so long to your own devices, my beautiful! But you asked for time, and I was generous. There were one or two matters I could attend to, but now—now I am going to take you where we shall not be disturbed, not even by thoughts!" He strode rapidly across the room and touched the wall.

A door flew open disclosing a narrow flight of steps. Iva was amazed, for only a second ago she had been searching that part of the wall.

Leaving the door open, the Great Mind came to Iva and picking her up as though she were a baby, carried her through the door. Then he paused a second on the top step and pulled a lever. So far as Iva could see, nothing happened.

Without delay he pulled another lever downwards, as he had the first. This time there were results for the door swung shut.

"So!" he cried, "We shall descend! No one will find us here!"

At that moment Iva knew her last hope was gone.

Chapter XXVII
Ota Meets Obstacles

When Gana's multan halted before the Golden Steps leading to the Palace, a long line of vari-colored men were waiting. Four rows deep they stood, silently, with Frathra at their head.

Gana delivered Ota's ultimatum and his promise of protection, just as the Blue Lord, himself, rode up.

The ranks of Gana's men divided and Ota, Noa, with Gotha and Erda, swept through until they were beside Gana, facing the Palace. The rest of Ota's personal guard mingled with Gana's men in the rear.

In response to Gana, the Great Mind's Lieutenant said, "It is difficult to believe these things you say."

"Yet they are true."

Now Ota broke in wearily, "We waste time, but show him, friend Noa. Perhaps one of his men will volunteer."

A low murmur of dissent rose among the ranks. Noa dismounted and walked to a nearby tree. "Behold this tree!" he cried, and turned the blue ray upon it. In one second the magnificent object was no more.

Quietly Noa resumed his place by Ota's side while the vari-colored men shouted acclamations for the Blue Lord.

As the last echoes died away, Frathra came forward. Close to Ota he stood and spoke firmly. "We accept your offer, oh, Blue Lord, and become your men, relying on your protection. Now I have a message for you from the Great Mind."

"Speak on!" Cried Ota.

"Your Father bade me give you his greetings and to tell you that he has retired to his secret chamber with the Earth Girl."

A groan that he could not repress forced itself between Ota's lips.

Frathra went on. "He said further that when he was ready he would come forth to greet you, also that you cannot hope to find them, even if you should demolish his Palace, which, if you were foolish enough to do, would put an end forever to your erstwhile Lady."

As Frathra spoke the last words, Ota raised his hand as though to strike the vari-colored man; but before he could lower his arm, Noa spoke.

"The words are not his, my Lord."

Ota's arm dropped heavily to his side. "I am half distracted, when I think of my Lady." He turned to Frathra. "Can you not take me to the secret chamber?"

"I know it not, my Lord. There is no one who has ever seen it. I know it must have entrance into the Great Mind's inmost chamber, but beyond that my knowledge does not go."

"Then take us to the inmost chamber at once!" Ota slid off his multan. Noa and Erda followed suit. Gotha started to dismount, but Ota stopped him. "Stay, my friend, and gather my people together when they come. Take their weapons from them. The blue ray is too powerful to be lightly handled. Save but your own and those of your brothers, I do not want a tube unaccounted for. Collect the rest and put them into chests, lock them and keep the keys for me."

Gotha raised his right arm. "To hear is to obey."

"I take Gana and two of my own men with me," Ota announced as he started to follow Frathra up the steps.

Noa walked beside his Lord while Erda followed with the other men.

Just as they reached the top of the steps and were about to enter the doors, the group of Blue People escorting Efa rode up.

Gotha, seeing the old woman, called out to Ota to stop.

The Blue Lord, too far away to distinguish faces or hear actual words, sent one of his men back with orders that if anything important had happened, to follow after him with whatever news there was. Then he plunged on with his followers.

Now that he was so near to the girl he loved, he could wait for nothing. His one desire was to get to Iva. He had given up hope that he would be in time to save her, and the thought dragged on his heart as a heavy weight might have done. But, even though he could not save her, he would at least be able to release her, and in his arms she would find comfort.

The little party, under Frathra's guidance, drew up before the door through which not so long ago the Earth Girl had been thrust.

"This is the entrance to the Great Mind's inmost chamber. How to gain admittance, I cannot tell. The door has always been opened from the inside." Frathra's voice died away into silence.

"Frustration! Frustration always!" cried Ota. "Is there no way?"

The vari-colored man shook his head.

"The blue ray, my Lord," came from Noa.

"I am afraid. Suppose it goes far enough beyond the door to reach my Lady?" Ota's voice broke.

"The message was, they were in the secret room, not here."

Then Frathra addressed the guards who were still at their places at either side of the door. "Did you hear aught within?"

They shook their heads.

"They know naught of the secret room," Frathra stated.

"There is no choice left. I must chance the ray." Ota pulled the tube from his belt and retreated as far back as he could go, the others keeping with him.

Levelling his weapon at the door, he was about to release the shield when the man he had sent back arrived with Efa.

The old woman flung herself at Ota's feet. "My Lord, my Lord!" she cried, "Where is my Lady?"

"In the secret room, wherever that can he," Ota told her curtly. Now was not the time to ask for explanations. His one desire was to find Iva.

"I know where it is! If you can take me inside the inmost chamber, I can lead you to it, for once when I was one of his household, the Great Mind took me there, and I noted well the way!"

"By the Red Sun, your reward will be great! Stand back and I will demolish the door." Ota thrust the woman behind him and released the shield, then almost immediately pressed the button that put it back into place. The blue ray shone for only an infinitesimal part of a second, yet when they looked, the door was gone.

Efa chuckled. "Good magic, Lord Ota, but powerless without my knowledge." She laughed, a thin, reedy laugh. She was quite happy now, for the hour of her triumph was near at hand. Never had she thought things would be made so easy for her. She had hoped the Great Mind would take Iva to the secret room, but that he had actually done so and that she would see Ota's face in the hour of the crashing of his plans, was an added joy. She did not mind so much now the Ruler of Venus's possession of the Earth Girl. Her delight in the thought of Ota's disappointment was too strong for that.

They all rushed into the room.

"The door! Open the door!" Ota pushed the old woman forward.

"I am too short. See that carving that runs along just below the ceiling? There is a multan upon it. If you press somewhere in the locality of its head, the door will open."

Gana sprang forward. "The task is mine, my Lord. I am half a head taller than anyone." With his fingers he was already feeling the multan's head, pressing every available spot. All at once he felt something give under his fingers and knew he had found what he sought.

Two things happened. The hidden door swung open, revealing the flight of stairs, and at the same time the floor under Gana's feet gave way and he fell through into a great, gaping hole. He gave a shrill shriek as he disappeared from view—then there was an ominous silence.

Ota went to the edge of the opening. Far below he could see flames shooting up.

"The burning pit!" he cried.

"The burning pit!" Efa echoed, "and beside it is a room that the Great Mind had built so he could watch those whom he had sentenced, or wished to get rid of, going to their doom. One whole side of the room is transparent so he can see through. Later he used it for his love-making. The sight of the flames inspired him. So, at least, he whispered in my ear." Efa watched Ota's face and flung each word at him in concentrated hate.

Another time Ota would have noticed this, but now he ignored her and spoke to Noa. "I knew of the pit, myself. There are chutes to it from all parts of the Palace. We must find a way to cross over the opening and to descend the stairs."

The hole stretched a good twelve feet before them. On the other side was the stairway. But there seemed no possible way to bridge the gap.

"Try the couch," the Blue Lord commanded, and swept the cushions upon the floor, trying not to think of the sweet form that must so short a while ago have rested upon them.

Feverishly they worked to swing the heavy couch across the chasm. It bridged the gap, but when they rested it securely on the farthest side, it just touched the edge of the floor nearest them. The least jar and it would slide back and consign them to the flames.

"It must be held firmly on this end while we cross," Ota announced. Then he designated the task to two of his own men and the guards who had watched the door.

When the men had taken their positions, holding on securely to the legs of the couch, he drew a deep breath. "I go first!"

"Not so, my Lord! Your existence is too precious! Let me try." And before Ota could say yes or no, Noa had started.

Slowly, carefully, so that no lack of balance could disturb the precarious hold of the couch, he stepped across the flimsy bridge. As the couch was soft, Noa's feet sank deep into it with each step and his progress was necessarily slow, but at length he gained the far side and called across that it seemed safe.

Ota went next, following the same tactics. He had hardly landed upon the other side before Efa started. He called back for the others to come, excepting the men who held the couch, who were to wait for their return. Then without waiting to see how his instructions were obeyed, he started down the narrow stairs, closely followed by Noa.

The stairs stretched down interminably. It seemed to Ota they would never end. As they descended, it grew very warm. In fact, on the left side they could not bear to touch the wall.

"We come nearer to the burning pit," Noa stated.

Ota made no reply. He was hurrying down the narrow stairs as fast as possible.

They had gone down about two hundred feet when they saw far away a little level space, on the other side of which was a door. Even at this distance, Ota could discern that the door had a knob.

Here the Great Mind felt so safe that he had thought there was no need to create further protection for himself.

They went down another fifty steps. There were only about ten more, Ota thought, and thanked the Red Sun. The suspense and not knowing what he would find, was almost too much for him.

Just as he put his foot on the level space, he heard a scream. With mingled horror and joy he recognized Iva's voice.

Chapter XXVIII
Revenge

When the Great Mind sprang his trap and shut the door at the top of the stairs, he felt a flare of triumph. He might have lost his kingdom, but assuredly he was getting the best of his son!

Something of his exultation was in the kiss he gave Iva.

He carried her down the stairs leisurely. He felt quite safe. He knew that this son could not demolish the door without falling into the burning pit. He had observed that the blue ray did not carry a great distance, therefore Ota would have to stand on the trap if he brought his new weapon into use.

Besides, Ota would never know where to look for the entrance. No one in all Gecca knew.

The Great Mind had forgotten that once he had taken Efa to the secret room. Nor would he have been concerned had he remembered. He had no idea that Efa was in Gecca.

He had not thrown his mind back to hear Ota's words on receiving the message from Frathra. The Great Mind was not interested in hearing something that he could foretell easily. While Ota searched the Palace feverishly for a trace of the concealed door, he would be quite safe—safe until he chose to come forth.

As he went down, he explained to Iva about the burning pit. He did not tell her how many helpless victims of her own sex had been flung into its fires of late years. Nor did he mention that he intended a like fate for her.

Once he had no more use for the Earth Girl, he was going to throw her into the pit. Then he would either go back and tell Ota what had transpired, or stay in his underground quarters until he had discovered a weapon more powerful than the blue ray. In his laboratories he could easily do that.

He carried Iva through the door, which he did not even bother to fasten. Then he set her on her feet and proceeded to exhibit the room. He led her over to the transparent wall and made her look down into the burning pit.

Iva saw the leaping flames and wished she could throw herself into them. She felt more dead than alive, for once again she was robbed of hope. Ota could never find her here.

Slowly, as though he took a kind of joy in prolonging her agony, the Great Mind led her through his laboratories, rooms which opened out from the secret room and stretched on and on.

Holding her by the wrist, he dragged her through room after room, proudly boasting of the things he had done in them, the egomania in him craving expression and admiration.

At last he turned back. Now Iva began asking questions. Here, among all these crucibles, strange tubes and paraphernalia, she felt safe at least from his love-making.

"What is that?" She pointed to a huge apparatus.

"That is where I distill the magic fluid for the belts."

"Are the belts really life-giving?" Iva asked wearily, more for keeping the ball of conversation going than for any other reason.

"You are clever, you Earth People! You discern in a moment what my people will never know."

"You mean?"

"I mean that any idea which is firmly planted in the mind eventually becomes a fact. In the beginning I wanted a hold on my people, so I invented the belts. I told them they had magic properties—and they believed. Now without them they shrivel away and become—inanimate food for the burning pit—because they believe in the idea I have planted so firmly in their minds—that of the properties which actually do not exist."

Iva said nothing.

The Great Mind continued, "It is the same with you Earth people. You believe in death. There is actually no death. If you did not believe in it and expect it, the process would not happen. As it is, you only throw off your outer garment, as a bower bursts through its pod. The body is only an outer clothing but it is beautiful—beautiful as your body is beautiful!"

He looked at Iva and the light of desire burned in his eyes. It was stronger than his ego.

Try as she might, she could not get him talking again. He merely quickened his pace. She lagged back, and then he took her in his arms and carried her swiftly to the secret room.

"My beautiful!" he cried, "So beautiful—blooming for me alone! A flower that only I may wear. Come, give me your lips that I may drink of your sweetness."

For one awful moment she endured his caresses. Then she screamed.

Outside, Ota cried, "I am coming!" as he flung open the door.

The Great Mind leapt to his feet and held Iva in front of him.

Ota burst into the room, followed by Noa. "I come in time to revenge your wrongs, my Lady!" His voice trembled a little at the sight of her.

Gladness shone from Iva's eyes. "Ota! Ota!" Then as she rightly interpreted the sadness of his face, she stammered, "My Lord, my Lord, you are not too late."

A cry of joy came from Ota as he realized the significance of her words.

It was echoed by another cry, this time from Efa, who, closely followed by Erda, had crowded into the room. Only her cry was of disappointment, for she was cheated of part of her revenge.

All this time the Great Mind was using Iva as a shield, as he backed away towards the transparent wall.

Ota moved forward slowly, for he feared for the Earth Girl.

When the Great Mind reached the wall, he held Iva to him with only one arm. Then, with his free hand he felt along the wall until he found a button, which he pressed.

Quite suddenly the whole transparent part of the wall swung outward. Like a great drawbridge, it hung suspended on chains, out, over the burning pit. Instantly the room became unbearably hot.

For the first time the Great Mind spoke. "Never shall you possess her!" And still holding Iva against him, he backed out on the transparent wall that was now a floor under his feet.

But Ota had anticipated his design. With feet that had never moved more swiftly, he ran out upon the bridge and getting behind the Great Mind, grasped his two arms and pulled with all his strength, forcing the erstwhile Ruler of Venus to give up his hold upon the girl.

The sudden release threw Iva off her balance. She fell down in a little heap on the transparent floor.

Ota and the Great Mind began to struggle near the edge of the bridge. Below them Iva could see the flames—flaring more fiercely than ever, as though in expectation of a victim.

Iva remained where she was, watching the struggle, praying with all her strength that Ota would be victorious.

The two men swayed back and forth. Both magnificent specimens, they were perfectly matched antagonists, for although the Great Mind was no fighter and Ota was, still Ota's long ride and exertions—mental and physical—had wearied him so that they were about equal.

As they fought, Ota panted, "Surrender, my Father, and I will see that you—."

The Great Mind cut him short. "Never! Annihilation for one or both of us!" His breath came quickly.

They wasted no more time on words, only fought in desperation, while the others watched intent on the battle.

Noa fingered his weapon but the two figures were so closely interlocked, it was impossible to use the blue ray.

All this while Efa, unperceived, crept closer and closer to the Earth Girl. This was her moment! While the two men who wanted Iva fought for her possession, she, Efa, would hurl the Earth Girl down into the flames.

Revenge—REVENGE! Just as she had planned it! She drew nearer to Iva, then like a whirlwind, she was upon her, pulling the Earth Girl to her feet and pushing her towards the side of the transparent bridge!

Iva desperately caught hold of the chain by which the bridge hung suspended. She dared not cry out. If she did, Ota would look back and that one glance might cost him his victory.

She clung to the chain while she tried vainly to shake Efa loose.

Suddenly aid came. Erda, who loved her Lady more than any-one on all Venus, had been watching the battle and Iva at the same time. That is, she would look first at the struggling men, then back at her Lady, rejoicing in the fact that they had found her unharmed.

Now as she looked, she saw the Earth Girl clinging to the chain, with Efa trying hard to dislodge her hold to it.

Erda, who had always viewed Efa with suspicion, took in the situation immediately. She rushed forward and with one hand grasped Iva's belt firmly, while with the other she pushed the old woman with all her might. The attack being entirely unsuspected, and the Blue girl being strong, Efa was swept forward.

The old woman tried to regain her balance. She clutched at the chain, missed—then fell downwards into the burning pit. The flames closed over her body.

Erda stood still a second to regain her own equilibrium. Then she lifted Iva gently backwards.

The culmination of events focused suddenly upon Iva. She saw Efa hurled to destruction in a kind of daze. She let go of the chain as she felt she was being drawn backwards to safety, then looked up with a grateful smile at her rescuer.

"Erda," she breathed, trying to make her brain remember some-thing that she wanted terribly to do.

All at once she knew what it was. Ota was fighting—she must watch. She turned her head to see the fighting men, just in time to behold a body hurtling through space, down—down—into the leaping flames. To add to her terror, she could not distinguish who the survivor was!

Her eyes were growing dim—her head was swimming—

"Ota! Ota!" she called, and then fell back lifeless into Erda's arms.

Chapter XXIX
By the Red Sun

To Iva there was nothing in the world but pain—or so it seemed—pain all mixed up with heat. Her whole body seemed to be on fire. Surely she must be in the burning pit!

If so, where was Ota? She called his name over and over in a dry, parched voice that sounded curiously unlike her own. She kept calling, and after what appeared like ages, from somewhere came an answer, but she couldn't make it out. She tossed restlessly and tried to distinguish the words. But it was no use, nothing seemed to penetrate the pain which burned through her.

After a while, Iva stopped calling, and a kind of peace descended. Then the heat went away and a soothing coolness enveloped her. This was so pleasant that she ceased struggling—and sank into oblivion.

When she finally heard a voice breaking through the calm that surrounded her, she fiercely resented it.

"Iva, Iva," it kept on saying.

She did not want to open her eyes. She felt so peaceful she never wanted to have to think again.

But the voice went on, "Iva, Iva."

Finally it penetrated the wall with which she had surrounded herself.

She opened her eyes. Ota was bending over her.

Of course he must be dead, too. They were meeting as ghosts. But even so, the joy of beholding him was almost more than she could bear.

"Ota, I love you," she whispered.

She thought it strange that he looked at her sorrowfully. He should be happy now that they were together again. What did it matter if they were dead, as long as they were together? Perhaps he had forgotten what "I love you" meant, though she had told him.

She spoke again, in his own soft musical language, "Ia dowa sea."

Ota's expression was no longer sad. "Now do I truly give thanks to the Red Sun!" He dropped on his knees beside her and caught her up into his arms. "My Lady," he whispered.

His touch was real. "Are we not dead?" Iva cried, while her heart beat faster because he was near.

"No, my love, we are indeed alive, but for these many days your mind has been elsewhere; though you called me and I was close, you did not know me."

Now was Iva's turn to know joy. She flung both arms about Ota's neck. Their lips met and life began again for Iva.

Presently she stirred in his arms. "I thought you were in the pit. I was searching for you. I suppose I have had a fever."

"I knew it must be some disease of Earth's, and I could do nothing but wait—and hope. Each day was torment to me."

"My poor Ota. Never again will you suffer so! But tell me what happened—the Great Mind?"

Iva was quite herself again. Her body with its Venusian strength was as strong as ever—stronger than it had been on her own planet. Only her Earth mind had been affected by the long strain. Now all was well with her, and her love for Ota more overpowering than ever.

"Just as Erda rescued you from Efa's clutches, I succeeded in shaking off the Great Mind's hold. He, too, lost his balance and fell into the pit. A fitting end for him who had sent so many others thither," Ota said.

Iva breathed a sigh of relief.

The man she loved went on, "You lost consciousness. I carried you up the steps, and ever since Erda and I have watched over you. I left you at intervals only long enough to settle the affairs of Gecca.

"Tell me, Iva, shall we live in Gecca—or the Blue Land?"

Iva wasted no time in answering, "The Blue Land—I love the Palace of the Four Towers."

"Then I shall leave Noa here to fill my Father's place as my representative, and we shall go back to my own land which I, too, love. Erda will go, too, and be your woman always. She has earned the right." Ota smiled into Iva's eyes.

"I could not stay here, remembering. Oh, Ota, I am so glad— that you came—in time!" A shadow fell across Iva's face.

Ota wiped it away with his next words, "Do you know what day this is?"

Iva shook her head.

"The allotted time has passed. While you lay senseless here the days went by. This very hour I will take you to the Temple and claim you for my wife—and then—." In Ota's voice was a quality that brought the swift color to Iva's cheeks.

"And then?" she whispered, with her lips against his.

"And then, by the Red Sun, you shall be mine at last!"

Other Beyond Pulp Reprints

THIS IS LIFE: REDISCOVERED SHORT FICTION

FRANK LONDON BROWN

Between November 1959 and November 1960, Chicago writer Frank London Brown wrote "This Is Life," a series of very short stories for the *Chicago Defender*. These poignant, vibrant vignettes observed episodes of Black life in Chicago in Brown's trenchant style.

FETTERED AND OTHER TALES OF TERROR

GREYE LA SPINA

Although she's mostly forgotten now, in the heyday of the pulps, Greye La Spina was more commercially successful than H.P. Lovecraft. This volume is the single largest collection devoted to this unjustly neglected queen of pulp horror, containing three short stories, a novella, and a serial novel published in her first decade as a writer.

frombeyondpress.com

Other Beyond Pulp Reprints

THROUGH TIME AND SPACE WITH FERDINAND FEGHOOT

REGINALD BRETNOR

Between 1956 and 1992, under the name Grendel Briarton (an anagram of his real name), Reginald Bretnor wrote 122 very short sci-fi stories about Ferdinand Feghoot, a time-traveling, galaxy-hopping emissary from the Society for the Aesthetic Rearrangement of History. Each story is an elaborate setup for a pun. Back in print for the first time in 30 years, with new illustrations.

REQUIEM FOR A SIREN: WOMEN POETS OF THE PULPS

ED. JACLYN YOUHANA GARVER & MICHAEL W. PHILLIPS JR.

The first-ever anthology of sci-fi and horror poems published by women in pulp magazines in the first half of the 20th century contains work by Dorothy Quick, Lilith Lorraine, Mary Elizabeth Counselman, and more. Includes an introduction, poet bios, and themed essays.

frombeyondpress.com